The Best of
Faith, Fiction, Fun and Fanciful

Lynn Squire

The Best of Faith, Fiction, Fun, and Fanciful
Copyright © 2008 Lynn Squire
All rights reserved

Cover Illustration by Lynn Squire
Cover Design by Lynn Squire

Table of Contents

Where Freedom's Found

Acknowledgements

First and foremost, I must acknowledge the Savior of my soul. If it were not for His abundant mercy and grace, I would not be able to write as I have, and my life would be bitter and vile. By His goodness, I have found freedom, and by His grace, I have found joy. To God be all the glory, honor, and power forever more.

I must acknowledge the wonderful husband my gracious Heavenly Father has given me. God used this humble and patient man to transform my life—I never thought I'd have it so good. Thank you, honey, for being willing to see my heart and help me on my journey.

Of course, I must say thanks to those three wonderful blessings who love to listen to me tell stories of my childhood. I couldn't have asked for more perfect children. Thank you for all your inspiring antics and thoughts.

Thank you, Nikki Bolton, for giving of your time to help with the editing process. Thank you, my awesome ACFW critique group for putting up with my emotional hiccups and for your gracious words of encouragement. God used each one of you to help me grow. Thank you, FCW Intense and FCW Basic Critique Groups, your exceptional critiques improved my writing and taught me so much. Especially thank you to Vicki McCollum, for your faith in me and perseverance. Your hard work and great insight stretched me and challenged me.

Then to my parents and my sisters, whose unwavering faith held my goal in sight. Thank you as well, my very supportive mother-in-law, your experience and wisdom helped me hone my skills.

And thanks to those loyal readers of my *Faith, Fiction, Fun, and Fanciful* newsletter who have stuck by me. Without you this would not exist. Thanks also to each reader who purchased this book, without you I could not continue.

May God use this short book to enrich your soul and bring a bit of pleasure, perhaps even great joy, to your pilgrimage.

Introduction

You have heard that life is a journey. We are born to a course somewhat set by the environment, culture, and ancestry within which we find ourselves. Will you join me on an exploration of this journey? *Faith, Fiction, Fun, and Fanciful* evolved from reflecting upon the paths of life I have journeyed and the lives of those I've met along the way. Some of those paths have led to periods of joy, some periods of sorrow, and some periods of remorse. These are the ways of life.

For the most part, we govern our pilgrimage by our desire for joy, love, peace, and the good things of life. We seek out places of inspiration and of safety. More often than not, we want to be coddled and cooed to, affirmed of our goodness, and held in a place where we are free from fear and pain and suffering. Yet, life holds more. If we cling only to those places of comfort we would never experience the true joy of success after hard work, or the true comfort of peace after a time of war. If we are not willing to risk it all for another, we would not understand or value true love. The hardships of life present to us a perspective of the good things that we would not have if we did not experience trials and sufferings.

This collection of short stories, poetry, prose, and devotionals takes us through the journey of life, its rises and falls, its joy and sorrow, and its moments of revelations. My prayer is that you gain the best in the end. May you enjoy the fanciful, have fun, be touched by the fiction, and grasp the faith.

God bless you all.

The

Human

Condition

The Briefcase

Harry Dunsbury pushed his glasses up his sweaty nose. One more customer and he would be done for the day. He wiped his brow with a cloth and pushed the "next customer" button by his seat. After this one, he'd count and balance his cashier drawer and head home. What would he do tonight? The usual, macaroni and cheese and a soft drink in the company of whatever happened to be on television. He sighed. His was a dull life.

A sleek, thirty-something man strode up to his window.

Harry's cheek twitched. This was the kind of man Harry dreamed to be, a man of great dapperness.

The gentleman slid a withdrawal slip through the window.

Harry wiggled his nose. Hardly anyone used these slips. He scanned the name, Clay Gainsworth. Withdrawal, $10,000. Harry's eyes bugged out. "Ah, excuse me sir, I need to get authorization to withdraw this amount."

The man nodded curtly and looked about the room. He touched his hand to his handkerchief neatly folded in a triangle in his suit jacket, and then slid his hand into his pants pocket.

Harry pushed his glasses up again and locked his drawer. He huffed as he pushed his heavy body off of the stool and wobbled to the manager's office. Within a few minutes he was counting out $10,000 in one hundred dollar bills to Clay Gainsworth, the man with the designer suit. At least it looked like a designer suit to Harry. He never actually saw the label, but it looked sleek, and it fitted the man well so it had to be.

The man nodded his head covered with dark hair.

Harry ran his hand over his smooth head and nodded back.

Mr. Gainsworth turned on his heel as though gliding and, with briefcase in hand, left the bank.

Harry stood at his teller window mesmerized. What would it be like to have that much money? What would he spend it on?

"Harry, you going to close up now?" Mrs. Tabort's squeaky voice interrupted his musing.

He sniffled, wiggled his nose, and twitched his lip. There ought to be a law against high-pitched voices.

He closed his window and removed his money drawer.

Having that much money would give him freedom from this bank, freedom to start that Internet business he dreamt of, selling movies online. He walked to the backroom and balanced his drawer. Maybe in some other lifetime.

Thirty minutes later, Harry said goodnight to the guard at the door and walked to the coffee shop around the corner. Stopping at the door, he gasped to catch his breath. Someday maybe they'd invent moving sidewalks and walking won't be necessary. With his breathing under control, he headed to the counter and bought himself a low-fat latté with a shot of butterscotch. *Nothing beats that.*

He settled down at a table and let the steam drift over his face, fogging up his glasses. As he removed them from his nose, he noticed a tall man sitting at the table by the door. The man stared out at the street as if waiting for someone. Harry put his glasses on and sure enough, it was Clay Gainsworth, the man from the bank.

Harry's gaze went to the floor where it landed on the briefcase. Such a nice briefcase, black with silver trim. And inside it—*wow, $10,000 dollars.* He mouthed the words.

Mr. Gainsworth stood, patted his handkerchief pocket, picked up his case, and strode out the door. Harry followed him, not really sure why. Perhaps he'd learn how rich men lived. Perhaps Mr. Gainsworth was up to some underhanded business. Whatever the man was about, it would certainly be more interesting than macaroni and cheese and whatever game show happened to be on the television. He hobbled out the door and down the street, puffing with each step.

Even though traffic whizzed by, Harry felt as though he and the dapper man ahead of him were the only people on earth.

Mr. Gainsworth turned down the alley.

Harry's mouth turned to a thought-filled frown as he came up to the alley. Pressing his hand against the wall, he peered around the corner. What business would such a suave man have in a dark alley?

Mr. Gainsworth's stride took an uneven gait. He clutched his chest and dropped the briefcase.

Oh no, the money! Harry hurried as best his short, fat legs would let him.

Mr. Gainsworth collapsed to the ground just as Harry reached him.

Harry pushed the briefcase under a discarded box and jumped as another man, punching his cell phone with his index finger, came running toward him.

"Hello, send an ambulance to the alley behind West California Bank on Springs Road. A man is down and I think he's having a heart attack." The stranger dropped to his knees beside Mr. Gainsworth. "Yes, I'll stay on the line." He turned to Harry. "Do you know CPR?"

Harry cringed. When did he last take that class? Was it two years ago? He nodded, not liking the idea of touching a strange man, even if he did know his name.

"I'm putting my phone on speaker. You do mouth to mouth and I'll pump."

Harry moistened his lips. His stomach turned as he stared at Mr. Gainsworth's once red lips, now turning blue.

"Hurry man, we don't have much time."

Harry tilted the dying man's head, closed his eyes and did his civic duty, praying the ambulance would get there quickly and he wouldn't catch some horrible disease.

What seemed like an eternity, Harry discovered, was really only a matter of minutes. The ambulance attendants took over the patient, and Harry stood back wiping his lips over and over and over again. His stomach threatened to expel his afternoon snack. This was not what he had planned when he followed his dashing hero.

When the ambulance drove away, the other man returned to the street.

Harry glanced at the box concealing the briefcase. What should he do with it? If the man died, who would know where it went to? Should he take it back to the bank? He glanced at his watch. The bank closed thirty minutes ago.

He took a deep breath and pushed over the box. The briefcase lay on its side, black as night with its silver trim shining in the growing darkness. He stretched out his hand and closed his fist. It wouldn't hurt to take it home with him. In a flash his hand grasped the handle. He sucked in air. It wouldn't hurt.

On the move again, he hustled to his building, climbed the two flights of stairs to his apartment, and stood panting as he fiddled with his key. The bolt clicked, and he rushed inside. *Please let no one have seen me.* He leaned against the closed door with his hand over his heart as though pressing it would stop the pounding.

The briefcase grip burned against his hand. He released it, and the case fell to the floor with a thud. Pushing it against the wall with his foot, he eyed it warily as he made his way to the cupboard. He would have to decide what to do with it later.

That night, Harry lay in bed. He pictured himself in Hawaii, lying on the beach, drinking pineapple-guava juice. Then he found himself in the most wonderful mansion ever built, with floor to ceiling windows, and plenty of servants to do his pleasing. The strain of the day pulled at his consciousness and he drifted away on a yacht through the Mediterranean . . . .

The captain of his yacht pulled into a cove of an island just off the coast of Greece. "There be the Isle of Golden Treasure, sir."

Harry's gaze followed the captain's finger to an island skirted by glorious coral rock peeking through the splashing waves.

"Beneath that coral, they say, lies treasure of unknown measure, but those that dive for it lose their souls." The captain shut off the engines and signaled for the anchor to be dropped. "Never been a diver return from this cove that hasn't told a sad tale."

"I don't plan to dive."

The captain nodded. "Just as well."

"I found a map that tells of a great treasure on the island. I plan on finding it." Harry looked up and saw his man walking toward him. "José! Is the speedboat ready, and do you have the map?"

"Si, Señor. I have it right here, but I must caution you once more Señor Dunsbury, this is not a place for a man of your dapperness to go."

Harry waved the compliment aside. "José, I was meant for this expedition. The lovely ladies back home will be disappointed if I don't follow through on my mission. We mustn't let their faith in me down."

"Your courage inspires me, señor."

"Then let us be on our way." Harry turned to the captain and tipped his Panama hat. "Good day to you, Captain. I'll see you before the sun sets."

"My best to you, sir." The captain stepped close to Harry, and whispered in his ear. "Are you carrying, sir? You don't know what vile creatures you'll meet on that island, and most certainly the Countess Tabort will not want you near her fortress at the top of Mount Goel." He pointed to the wall that circled the top of the island's tallest hill.

Harry placed a strong hand on the Captain's sleeve. "You know I always take my Colt with me wherever I go. She'll not give me trouble. I've dealt with her before. However, if something does go wrong, I'll signal with a flare." He pulled out a flare gun from his back.

The Captain nodded. They clasped hands and pounded each other's shoulders. "Good luck."

"Thanks, Captain." Harry scanned the rugged terrain. "I'll need every bit I can get."

In a flash, Harry and his trusted man José reached the shore. They clamored to hide the boat on the sandy beach beneath palm branches.

"The map!" hissed Harry.

"Si Señor." José pulled it from his shirt.

Harry scanned the map he had found in the briefcase. As best he could tell, it led to the buried money Clay Gainsworth had squirreled away from helpless widows over the years. "We'll have to climb this ridge, see? And get past that open field."

"I've brought the shepherd's costumes as you asked, señor." José handed him a plain robe. "I must warn you, there is a snake pit filled with vipers. You'll not get by it."

"Did you bring the rope?"

"Si."

"We'll get by, just follow my directions."

They climbed the ridge and skirted around a grove of olive trees. Stopping before a road, Harry scanned the area for sheep. By a stone bridge, on the other side of a small vineyard, grazed a small herd. Donning his robes, he waved for José to follow him. The widows' fortunes must be restored.

A car came over the hill.

He ducked beneath the bridge and peered around the corner. The villainess Countess Tabort must be in cahoots with Clay Gainsworth, for she drove the car. Harry and José would need to move with great care to avoid her hawk-like eyes. Creeping under the bridge and up the side of streambed, he and his man took the stance of shepherds, confident their disguise would fool the wicked woman.

"Señor, she turns around!"

"Quickly man, head for the brush!"

They ran, shedding their costumes and leapt behind a rosemary bush.

"Look, Señor, the snake pit!" José's voice quaked with fear.

Harry felt certain buried money lay on the other side of the pit. They must get around it or the widows would be doomed.

"Throw me the rope José!" Harry gritted his teeth. *We'll get that money, even if I must lose my life to do it!*

Harry grabbed the rope and tied it to the strong roots of the rosemary bush. He tied a spike to the other end and cast it across the pit. It hit the ground, lodging against a rock. With a sharp tug, Harry tested its stability. "José, I am going to walk across the rope. Stand guard."

"Señor, you are too brave."

"Yes, but I used to be a tightrope walker. I've not lost that skill."

"Si, senor."

Harry stepped out on the rope. With arms out and eyes up, he walked across the rope as though striding along a wide path. Around an unusually knotty tree, the map said, would be the money, buried beneath a rock.

At the bottom of the hill stood a tree of amazing size. He slid down the incline and stared at the shape of the tree's knots, each one larger than the head of a lion. A quick survey of the terrain and he soon found the stone. He must be quick or the Countess will descend upon him. With his powerful shoulders, he pushed the stone over and discovered a wooden chest.

Rubbing his hands together, he couldn't wait to get that money. He took his Colt and slammed the butt against the padlock on the chest. The lock fell to the ground.

His heart pounded. With great care he eased open the lid and peered inside. *Green. Beautiful green.*

The widows will love him.

He closed the lid and threw the chest over his shoulder.

The papers will praise his bravery. He'll write his story. Movies will be made about his grand expedition. But first, he must return to his yacht and make a safe sail to America.

15

With the agility of a gymnast and the strength of a weight lifter he carried the chest past the tree, up the steep hill and onto the tightrope.

"Stop right there, you nave!" Countess Tabort's screeching voice pulled him to a halt. "You'll not get away with this."

Harry looked over his shoulder. His foot slipped, but he countered the loss with his arm.

The Countess held a machete in her hand, raised and ready to drop on his rope.

He glanced down.

Vipers held high their heads. It was certain death. There was but one hope. He must bolt to the end and toss the chest to José.

Taking a deep breath, he pushed off the balls of his feet, and with the cat like moves of a ninja he raced.

The rope slackened.

He lifted the chest in the air and heaved it toward José. *For the widows!* He fell, his arms flaying in the air as he tried to grab the rope. *No!* He missed and down he fell into the pit. The snakes dove for him, biting him, biting him, biting him . . . .

Harry sat up, gasping. His eyes flew open.

His bed stood beside him. Something dug into his buttocks. Reaching underneath himself, he pulled out a remote control.

The biting vipers. He wiped the sweat off his face and laughed. It was only a dream.

He pushed himself off the floor. Tomorrow he would go to the hospital and find Clay Gainsworth. This hero business was a tad bit too dangerous for his liking. The briefcase was not his to keep.

The next morning, Harry eyed the case. It sat propped up against the wall where he kicked it last night, yet it had taken him on an adventure he never wanted to experience again.

After brushing his teeth, cleaning his glasses and shaving, Harry put on his Sunday suit and picked up the briefcase. He may not be rich, nor will he likely ever be, but at least he could try to look the part. Locking his door behind him, he strode down the hall to the elevator. Perhaps he'd stop by one of those gyms today and sign up. Maybe even go on a diet.

He rode the elevator down, caught a cab to the hospital, and with the confidence that Mr. Clay Gainsworth would exude, he walked up to the nurse. Within minutes, he stood by Mr. Gainsworth's bed.

The dapper man didn't look so dapper anymore, but his hair still looked grand. Tubes came out all over him; nonetheless, the nurse did say he could talk. "Mr. Grainsworth, sir, I have your briefcase."

"Oh, good man." He coughed. "I thought it was gone for good." He lifted a shaking finger and pointed at it. "Would you open it up? I want to be sure everything is in order."

"Of course, sir." Harry set the briefcase on the bed tray and popped it open. Inside it laid a new Mac notebook, super thin and super light. He ran his hand over it. This was better than money. What he could have done with something like this. He cleared his throat.

"My Mac notebook in there?"

"Yes sir."

Mr. Gainsworth let out a long sigh. "That's my life. All my stocks, bank records, and personal financial information are on that. Not to mention my business's secrets."

"Glad I found it for you, sir." Though admittedly, he wasn't sure how glad he was that he didn't keep it.

"Be a good man, would you." Mr. Gainsworth coughed. "I need to email my associates in Boston. Do you think you could get the wireless set up? My cell phone is in the drawer."

"No problem sir, I'm a wiz with computers."

In no time, Harry proved his words. Not only did he get the gentleman set up, but he helped him solve some issues with the new software Mr. Gainsworth had purchased.

He spent the rest of the morning by the gentleman's bed, helping him. By noon the nurse chased him out, but not before Mr. Gainsworth offered him the opportunity of a lifetime, to be a partner in his very successful Internet business.

Haystack Reverie

I slip through the barbed wire fence where it joins the bare rails of the corrals. Running my hands along the middle rail, I am reminded of a piece of driftwood, worn smooth by the polishing caress of the ocean, with just its knots left untouched.

Carried on the cool breeze is the familiar aroma of horse and cow manure. On the next wave of air comes the wonderful scent of horse sweat, a clear sign that today is hot for late August. The breeze ruffles my hair and I pull my cap over it before moving toward the haystack.

Beneath my feet, the brown grass crunches. I move to the well-worn tire tracks where the grass never recovered after many loads of hay crushed it. Dust puffs up around my feet, but is gently blown aside before it reaches my ankles. I stop to watch the grasshoppers hop and fly by like little helicopters heading off to pick up or drop off troops in a war zone.

The clanging of metal and the muffled voices of men working around machinery filters through the windbreaks and Caragana trees. To my right, horses stomp a steady beat, like a marching troop, as they methodically battle against the ever-present flies. To the left, a bull lets out a mournful bellow and is answered by another. A whirlwind whips grass and dust, and brings the fragrance of freshly cut hay.

I grab a bale. Its twine slashes my palms, and the hay scratches my knuckles. Like huge building blocks, I move these rectangular bales. They will make a staircase to the top of the stack. Placing the last bale, I startle a mouse that scurries away, only to be chased by my big sandy-colored dog, Mutt.

Once on top of the stack, I survey the land. For miles around, golden wheat fields spread out like shag carpet. In the distance, the snow-capped mountains jut out from the ground like dog's teeth. Overhead, a hawk cries then swoops down; perhaps after the mouse I scared earlier. Like a black wall, dark clouds rest in the north, threatening to fall upon us.

I hear a cry for help. As a superhero, I must respond. I run along the top of the stack, hopping from one bale to the next. A bale rocks, and I stumble, catching myself on the next. Up again, I continue to race to the call. With a mighty leap, I fly off the stack. Tucking my head to my knees, I flip and land on my back in a pile of hay. A cloud of dust and dry alfalfa leaves rise at my landing and then slowly float down in a salute to my bravery.

Some leaves land on my tongue, tasting like dry herbs, and I recall that it is time for supper. I push myself off the soft, yet scratchy bed of hay and hurry away just as the supper bell starts to ring.

The Man behind the Transformation of Ritland City

A Character sketch on greed and selfishness

"If I were Prime Minister," thought Theodore Ritland, "there would be no more unions." He turned from the window where he had been watching the picketers march in front of his building. His emotions wavered between anger, sorrow, and resentment.

"The fools!" Could they not see that he had nothing more to give? The money they claimed he held in an account in the Caribbean was for research and development. This should translate to job security and the creation of future employment for their children. "But they cannot see past their own selfish greed," he concluded.

Theodore sighed, his shoulders slumped, and he closed his eyes. The events of the past few months flipped through his mind like flashcards in a coiled book. The union representative made demands, and his associates had advised against giving into them. Theodore gave a little, but then the union wanted more—exactly as his associates said they would. He tried to help the people, yet they never seemed satisfied. How could he satisfy them? He clenched his teeth. His efforts were futile.

After a moment where his gut felt it would wrench from his body, Theodore stared at the conference room door. Negotiations were closing. The union would get what they wanted—higher wages, 100% dental insurance, and improved work conditions based on the five-year plan. Little did they know there would be no TR & Associates Mining Co. in five years.

Theodore suppressed the guilt that threatened his resolve. He had to take care of his own. It was now or never. Even a year from now the demands of the union would push him into personal bankruptcy.

He moved to his desk, picked up the telephone, and dialed. "Charles, sell the stock."

Computer keys clicked on the other end, and then a tenor voice cut the silence. "Done. The fifty million will be in your Swiss account by noon."

"Good." Theodore cradled the telephone. He took a deep breath, licked his lips, and strode into the conference room.

In minutes, the agreement was signed and the union got its demands. Theodore quelled the thoughts of sorrow for the city's future, or lack thereof, once TR & Associates Mining Co. closed. He stepped from the room, slowly closing the door behind him, with a sad smile. He'd taken care of his own, and that's what really mattered to him.

The Cold Truth about Timothy Laton

The most frightening person I ever knew was Timothy Laton. He was a tall, burly man with curly hair and an even curlier beard. He wore black boots—big, black boots—that stomped around, thundering anger from wall to wall no matter what building he was in.

My mother said he lost his wife, but the boys in school convinced me that he murdered her. He carried a rifle around where ever he went. Mom said he was a hunter. I always wondered what he hunted.

One evening I was ice skating at the old rink. Dad was late to pick me up, so I sat on the edge of the rink with my skates hanging around my neck. I was sliding my white snow boots back and forth, forming two ski-like prints, when Timothy Laton's big, black boots crunched snow behind me.

Startled, I jumped up, crushing the ski prints, and stood trembling in those white boots, now frozen to the ground.

He stopped, his large frame shadowing the wooden gate to the rink and me.

That is when I saw it. In Timothy's arms, wrapped in a warm wool blanket, was a whimpering Border Collie pup.

My eyes grew wide with fear for it, and my mouth froze shut in mute anger when I thought of what he might do to it. I imagined he would kill the dog in cold blood before me, like the boys told me he did to my Uncle Bob's cat.

Then I saw Timothy's big, black hand reach into his pocket, and I thought he was going to pull out that hand gun the boys at school said he kept there. He slowly eased his hand from his pocket. It held a steaming baby bottle.

I let out a breath of relief.

After gently pushing the nipple into the puppy's mouth, Timothy said, without cracking a smile, "Your pa wanted a sheep dog pup. My dog died having this one. I've been nursing it for four weeks now. Figure your dad could take it."

He pushed the pup into my arms, and then turned on his heel. His big black boots crunched snow as they marched away, and I blinked after them. Right about then the headlights from my dad's pick-up truck lit up the path to the rink and Timothy's strong, gentle back.

I listened to Timothy's black boots crunch the snow, and it occurred to me, as I walked to my dad's truck, that my white boots crunched snow just the same.

Stepping into the truck, I watched Timothy turn the corner. I guessed the boys from school and I were wrong about this big, black, burly man.

Knock Down

"Yo, Anne, got a light for my joint!" Justin shouted across the school hall. He punched his friend and laughed as the two drifted to the doors.

Anne Kawalsky pushed her hair behind her ear and sighed, attempting to ignore the remark. A renegade brown lock swept across her eyes. She despised her dull, brown hair, but hated her attached ear lobes, even more. So why then did she continually push her hair behind her ear? Habit, plain and simple.

It never occurred to her that her ear lobes were ugly until the Basher told her so last summer in front of the cutest boy in high school—Justin, to be precise. She pulled the hair back over the ear and smoothed it.

"See you later, Mouse!" He called back at her, and then slapped his leg while roaring with laughter.

Anne frowned and wished she could hide like a rodent.

Looking up from her locker she saw Ariel laughing with none other than her arch enemy, Brenda the Basher. She closed her locker door and took a deep breath. Ariel, popular and beautiful, had inherited her mother's flare for life. She, on the other hand, had received a full dose of her father's timid, bland personality . . . mousy, her mother called it.

"Did you see Chuck at the party last night?" Brenda asked Ariel.

"Wow, did I ever. He was so high." Ariel swished her blonde hair.

Anne's lips formed a grim smile as she watched Ariel lean close to Brenda in a secretive manner. Trouble brewed, and she felt it pushing against her heart. Why did Ariel seek friendship with that bullish girl?

24

Ariel caught her gaze and smirked. "Don't wait for me, Anne. I'm going . . ." she glanced at Brenda, "shopping." The two girls burst into a volley of giggles as they linked arms and headed to the exit.

Anne ran her thumb along the edge of her biology textbook. What kind of shopping would send a person into a round of laughter? She watched their staggering walk as they pushed through the school doors and sauntered down the street, still bent in glee.

She smacked her tongue on the roof of her mouth. Brenda was a bad influence on Ariel, taking her to outlandish parties and such. That's what dad said, at any rate. She should do something. She took a tentative step to the door. Ariel was sure to fall into some sort of catastrophe.

A bump from behind sent her flying into the lockers.

Tears crept along the edges of her eyes.

Around her seniors laughed and chattered while banging lockers, but she focused on the school doors.

A whiff of wonderful cologne drew her attention to Mike, the quarterback. She quickly dropped her gaze to the floor and slipped around him. Her cheeks burned.

Should she go after Ariel? Brenda was sure to mock her.

She stood before the doors, clutching her books. People bumped against her as they pushed past and exited the school.

She stared at the sidewalk on the other side of the school's threshold as though it were a sea of turmoil not to be walked upon by mere mortals such as herself.

"Did you hear about Brenda Black?" A girl whispered to another as she walked past.

Anne looked up. She took a deep breath. Eavesdropping could provide much needed information, as experience had proven time and again. She peered around the school hall like a fugitive on the run, and then, with head bowed, followed the girl and her friend out the door.

"Tommy said she keeps company with Roland Durham, the drug dealer."

"No way!"

"Yeah, way! And did you see her eyes yesterday?" The girl stopped and pulled on her friend's sleeve. "She was definitely on a high."

"Wow. Have you . . ."

Anne stopped dead in the middle of the sidewalk. *Drugs!* Could it be possible? Ariel couldn't be that stupid . . . could she?

25

She scanned the streets, hoping to see her sister. A block ahead Ariel and Brenda turned into the alley behind the county library. Setting her books on the brick wall beside her, she gnawed on her lower lip. She heard once, when sitting at Ripley's Café, a group of boys talking about that alley. Dealer Alley, they called it, where the drug dealers sold their wares.

Anne wrinkled her brow. *Dealer Alley.* It rolled over her like a tidal wave. *Ariel's done a lot of stupid things, but drugs?* She wiped her sweaty palms on her jeans.

Her feet took two steps forward. *If she went for help, she may be too late, or made to look like a fool if nothing was going down.* Her feet stepped out in a steady rhythm. *Ariel could be in trouble.* Her footsteps stretched into a run.

Dodging a car, she raced over the crosswalk. She leapt over a cat that scurried past. As she turned the corner a dog barked and she jumped, her heart pounding. She hated dogs. They all terrified her.

Pulling to a stop, she scanned the alley for any sign of her sister and Brenda the Basher. There, around the corner of the library, she saw the distinct bedazzled pant leg of her sister disappear. What should she do?

The dog's barking grew louder. She glanced back as a little black Scottish terrier rounded the corner. Frightened, she bolted down the alley while the animal yapped after her.

Barreling around the building, she slammed into Brenda. A bag of white powder fell from girl's hand. "You idiot!" Brenda screeched.

The Basher took off.

Anne glanced at Ariel's ashen face, and she knew what Ariel had nearly done. Guilt wrote its name on her sister's face. "How could you be so stupid?" She screamed at her.

Ariel pointed a shaking finger at Brenda. "She has Momma's wedding ring."

Just then, the yippy terrier ran at Anne, latching on to her pant leg. Anne shook her foot at the dog. Rage exploded in her head, rage like she'd never experienced before. She shoved her sister against the wall and kicked at the dog.

The animal wouldn't let go.

No time to waste. Grabbing the dog by the scruff of its neck, she ripped it away and raced after Brenda with a speed she never knew she had. Heat soared through her veins as she tore through the alley and out on the street.

Horns blared. A police whistle blew, but Anne only saw the back of her enemy. She lunged for it, arms stretched out. Pain ripped into her leg as the dog latched on and slowed her flight. She wrapped her arms around Brenda's legs, pulling her down on the street as tires screeched around them.

"Are you two kids crazy?" shouted a man in blue pants.

Anne looked up to see a police officer bent over them. He pulled the dog off Anne's leg. She clung to Brenda, who squirmed to get away. Tears filled Anne's eyes as the pain from the dog bite heated up. "Sir, she sells drugs."

The policeman grabbed Brenda by the collar and jerked her up. The girl still clutched the bag of white powder close to her chest. "Looks like we're going downtown," the officer muttered as he slapped cuffs on the Basher and marched her to the sidewalk. Brenda hung her head, her face as red as a beet.

"Sir." Anne wrapped her arms around her shivering body. "She has my mother's ring."

Brenda, sullen and pale, handed over the gold symbol of an old marriage. Anne limped over and sat down beside the wall of Ripley's Café. Her leg throbbed and tears rolled down her face, but a smile played on her lips. She may be mousy, most would attest to that, but no one messes with her sister when she's on watch. Not unless they want a knock down by Anne the Annihilator.

She pulled her legs up under her chin and held them tight while her sister came, like a puppy with its tail between its legs, and sat down beside her.

"Thanks, Sis."

"No problem, Ariel." She gave her little sister a hug, and watched the patrol car pull up to the curb. "I'm here for you, all the way kiddo." She rubbed her nose. "Why did you use Mom's wedding ring?"

Ariel shrugged. "I didn't have any money left after playing poker last night with the guys."

Anne rolled her eyes. Did Ariel have problems or what?

"Mom doesn't wear it any more anyway, not since dad died."

Anne shook her head. "That's stealing."

Ariel nodded and stared at the street.

After a few minutes, Ariel chuckled, and Anne lifted her eyebrow. "What's so funny?"

"I never thought I'd see the day when you would tackle Brenda the Basher." Ariel boxed her arm. "There's more to you than I thought, big sister."

Anne just smiled. No senses letting her sister's praise go to her head. After all, every superhero must have her alter-ego.

Out of the Storm

"Aunty Bess!" Little Mary's excited voice came through the wood door.

Bess filled the last sack of her secret herbal mixture, sure to cure a frog of its croak—at least that's what she told her patients.

"Aunty Bess!" The door latch clicked, and Mary's feet pattered on the stone floor in the foyer.

Bess tied a knot in the twine around the sack and picked up her oil-slicked cloak. The rain was sure to come now, and there would be no stoppin' the storm once it hits.

Mary slid around the corner. Bess glanced at the biddy as she tied her bonnet under her chin. "What be the problem, girl?"

"Mrs. Kilgarriff," Mary huffed. "She be coughing something awful, and Mr. Kilgarriff—" she paused to catch her breath. "He sent a pigeon."

Bess tucked the sack of herbs under her arm, and then drew a muffler around her neck. She raised an eyebrow. "Go on biddy, you're wasting time."

Mary grabbed Bess's arm. "He asked you to come quickly." She pulled on Bess' cloak.

Bess smiled and laid her hand on the girl's shoulder. "Child, I'm on my way. Don't you worry none. Now go get your father. He's at the stable. Tell him to bring the buggy around. I'm ready to go."

Bess stepped out the door. A rain drop splattered on the cobble walk. She glanced at the clouds. There'd be trouble in those dark thunderheads.

Richard drove the buggy to her. He hopped out and gave her a hand up. "Sis, you be careful now. Sure you won't wait until the storm passes and let me drive?"

Bess knitted her brow and waved a gloved hand at him. "You're busy enough here. I've been driving a horse longer than you, and old Seany-boy is as steady as he is black. Don't you be worrying none about me."

Richard scowled at her, but Bess chuckled. He never could see fit to let her be.

"You mind the road by Clonakilty, it gets powerful muddy when it rains." He grunted. "'Tis a shame they haven't got that fixed."

Bess shook her head and clucked at him. "Now I know what you are thinking, Richard, and Mr. Kilgarriff has all he can handle just trying to grow enough potatoes on that rocky land to feed their brood. He's as hard a working man as you."

Bess lifted the reins and kissed at the horse. "You mind my hens are locked up now, Richard. And Mary, you make a good stew for your father."

Bess stole a look at the clouds as the black gelding trotted off. She mightn't get pass Clonakilty before the heavens unleashed their fury on her.

The wind picked up as the buggy followed the ridge along County Cork's coast. Seany-boy trotted out strong, but Bess still felt the tide of anxiety work its way onto the shores of her heart. She tugged her bonnet tighter, down upon her ears. "Dear God, now you know Mrs. Kilgarriff needs these herbs. Make my way clear, if You see fit."

A clash of thunder answered her prayer, and the sound rumbled past the buggy. Seany-boy pulled the buggy up past Clonakilty and onto the long dirt road to Kilgarriff's Farm.

A splat of rain hit Bess' gloved hand. She gripped the rein. "Not going to wait are you?" she spoke to the gloomy sky.

In answer the clouds opened up and unleashed a flood of rain. Seany-boy snorted and tossed his head.

"Thank you Lord, for covered buggies." Bess leaned deeper under the top.

Seany-boy slipped.

Her heart jumped to her throat. "Steady, my boy. Steady."

She leaned forward to peer down at the road. A blast of wet wind met her, and she drew back. Her face stung from the rain that hit it.

She scowled at the storm. "Lord, now ye know it's important I get there. Those wee children, they need their mother."

Ahead rivers of water raced down the ruts in the road. She steered Seany-boy out of the ruts, gripping the reins as though her clasp could help the gelding keep its footing.

The buggy slipped.

Bess held her breath as she watched Seany-boy brace against the traces.

The buggy shaft banged the gelding's shoulder, and Bess winced in sympathy. "Keep going old boy. You're all right."

The horse dug his hooves into the wet ground, but then slid further to the right.

Bess gasped and gripped the dash rail in front of her. "Lord, I beseech thee!"

The buggy's back wheel skidded into the ditch. Bess clenched her teeth and pulled on the reins. "Whoa! Seany-boy."

The wind drove the rain hard into her face. She winced, no longer able to duck under the top for cover as the buggy now faced the storm head on.

The gelding stopped and stomped his feet. Its body trembled.

Water soaked through her bonnet, and Bess chided herself for not putting Richard's rain hat on instead. "Vanity. That's what that was, pure and simple vanity."

Bess huffed and pulled a handkerchief from her pocket. Wiping her face, she surmised was futile. While tucking the delicate cloth back into her pocket, she stepped down from the vehicle.

"Lord, now how am I to get to Mrs. Kilgarriff if I'm stuck in the ditch?" She placed her hands on her hips, and puffed at the sight of the mud covered horse and buggy.

A blast of wind pushed her forward.

She caught herself against the front wheel.

"Best get you out of this mess, Seany-boy." She hefted up her skirts and stepped down the sharp slope of the ditch, expecting to slip, but didn't.

"Now you stand still." Bess placed one hand on the wheel and reached forward to unhook the traces from the single tree.

Seany-boy slipped and the buggy shifted.

Bess' heart went to her throat. She lost her footing and slid down between the wheel and the legs of the horse. "Whoa!"

She exhaled with force. "Now that's just great." Taking care not to startle the gelding, she eased herself back up the side of the ditch. Her gloved hands were wet and cold to the bone, not to mention muddy.

Once on the road, she frowned. "Lord, what am I to do? Ye gave me this gift of fine herbs, and an understanding of how they work, and now there be a sick mother, who Ye know more than anyone needs my concoction, and yet here Ye are letting me get in this fix."

The thunder clashed in response. She refrained herself from shaking her fist at the Almighty. Not that she didn't feel she had good reason. She shook her head. "No sense wastin' my time arguing with you, Lord."

Grabbing the rein below Seany-boy's bit, she tugged on it. "Come on old boy, try to pull it out."

The horse lunged forward, but the breast collar halted him like a brick wall.

Her eyes widened as she watched the buggy shift.

The horse snorted and paddled his feet, struggling to find a hold on the ground. He fell to his knees.

She dropped to her knees too. "Oh Seany-boy. I got you into this. I'm sorry old boy."

Looking up at the sky, she blinked away raindrops that clung to her eyelashes. "Lord, Ye know I'm a stubborn woman, but would Ye have that Mrs. Kilgarriff should die if I donna get these herbs to her?"

The thunder crashed and a gust swatted the flap of her cloak against her face. She pulled the wet muffler about her neck off. "I be a fool, I know."

Lightening sliced the horizon. The Lord be the Creator, after all. Should not He know and ensure the fate of those He loves?

The waves crashed against the rocks on the beach below.

"Who am I, Lord, that I should be so bold?" She pushed a wet strand of hair from her forehead and stood. "Best get a cover for you, Seany-boy."

She slipped down the side of the ditch to the vehicle. "Now, there's usually a wool blanket in the chest under the seat."

The harness jingled, and she glanced at the horse. It lowered itself to its knees, knocking against the shaft and pushing the buggy into a more precarious position.

"Ah Lord, Let me at least help my animal!" She shot an anxious look at the heavens before taking a further step.

Reaching deep into the vehicle, she unlatched the chest. Rain ran between her collar and her neck, and rolled down the skin of her back. She shivered. *Perhaps there is a canvas as well to cover me self,* but as she reached further, the buggy tipped.

She grabbed the blanket and leapt back. Just as she moved away, the shaft by the gelding snapped, and the buggy rolled onto its side.

Seany-boy whinnied and scrambled as the traces pushed against the horse's side.

"Lord, help him!" She watched with her heart in her throat as the buggy-horse fought against the straps, further entangling itself.

The single tree snapped from the vehicle. The horse snorted and Bess gasped.

She clambered out of the way while Seany-boy struggled to get free from the harness and the buggy. The horse leapt forward, and the shaft pulled free from the tug, releasing the animal.

Bess rushed to grab the reins as the gelding bounded up the ditch. It stopped on the road, head down, sides heaving, and legs shaking.

"There old boy," she soothed as she climbed up beside the horse. Looking overhead at the tumbling storm clouds she said, "We're in the Lord's hands now."

The gelding's hind legs crumpled. Bess jumped out of the way as the horse collapsed.

Her heart wrenched. She hated to see the animal suffer. Laying the wool blanket over its body, she grumbled, "What a prideful old fool I've been, Seany-boy."

Bess knelt in the mud by the horse's head and stroked the damp fur behind its ears. "Truth be known, I pride myself in helping others at the risk of hurting those I love."

She studied the sky. The torrential rain changed to a drizzle, and she pulled the collars of her cloak up around her neck. "'Tis a shameful thing, Lord, I know. Here I claimed I was so indispensable, forgetting You're the Almighty."

She stared down at the muddy road as self-reproach washed over her like the run-off.

Seany-boy snorted. Bess looked at him.

She heard the squeaking of saddle leather and looked up to see her sweet brother riding up behind her.

She started to fuss over her appearance, and then stopped. Was that not pride creeping in again?

"When the storm came in so fast I worried." Richard spoke with a gentle voice. He dismounted.

Bess stood. "I was foolish to go."

Richard waved a hand at her, and knelt down at Seany-boy's back. He studied the horse for awhile.

Bess ran her hand over her face, as though it would wipe away the remorse.

"He'll be all right," Richard said as he got back on his feet. "I'll stay with him. You take my horse. The storm's let up, you'll be safe enough."

Bess lifted a prayer of thanks for such a kind brother. "'Fraid my herbs are in the buggy."

Richard looked over the edge of the ditch and shook his head. "Not safe to go down now. We'll have to wait 'til it dries."

"But my herbs, Richard." Tension rose behind Bess' eyes, and she rubbed her temples.

"You go on now. God's the Healer, not you."

Bess closed her eyes and nodded. She had to admit he was right, though it hurt to acknowledge it. Oh, dash her tendency toward self-importance. She glanced to the heavens. *Forgive me once more, dear Lord.*

"I'll give you a leg up."

Bess rode for another five miles through the cold wet rain. When she arrived at the Kilgarriff's house she was glad for the warm fire. What warmed her heart though, was to see Mrs. Kilgarriff sitting up in bed, the fever gone.

Bess spent the next few days caring for the needs of the family while Mrs. Kilgarriff got her strength back. But more than that, she spent each day thanking the Lord for teaching her who was really in control.

Prodigal Farmer's Daughter

"She ought to be held accountable for her actions." Jerry slammed the hammer against the fencing staple, driving it deeper into the fence post. Five years of free and easy living, and her sister is welcomed home with the red carpet rolled out.

Jerry had slaved beside Father to hold the farm together after Mother died. Corrie, the renegade, chose instead to run off to the city to become a professional model. Jerry placed her hand on her hip and held a mock pose. She shook her head and snorted. For five years, they never heard from Corrie. Jerry swung the hammer with the strength of her fury.

The top wire now in place, she rolled the barbed wire out on the ground for the next line.

Nothing could exonerate Corrie's behavior. "Dad not only lost a wife, but also a daughter that year."

Jerry snatched up the wire stretcher. The hook swung around and banged her knee. Sharp pain crumpled her leg. She yelled and kicked the stretcher, which only made her toe hurt. What a stupid thing to do.

Stupid? What was stupid was letting Corrie come home. Jerry stared at the fence post. "Out of money, in rags, and smelling like a pig, she saunters into the house as though nothing was wrong." Jerry spat. "After five years of worry and what does Dad do? Welcomes her with open arms! He takes her shopping for new clothes, and takes her to all her favorite restaurants in town, while I slave here in the hot sun!"

Jerry hooked up the wire stretcher and gave it a good yank. She'd always been the faithful, hardworking Jerry. She twanged the wire to test for tightness before hammering in the fencing staples. Hadn't Dad said he could always depend on her?

Glancing at the sun, she set her tools down and walked to the truck for her lunch. Dad and Corrie would be sitting down at the top of the Calgary Tower, watching the world go by as the restaurant revolved. Why couldn't she have gone?

She bit into the rough rye bread sandwich and jerked her head back, tearing the meat inside.

A cow and a calf ambled down to the spring at the bottom of the coulee. The Red Angus calf dashed into the creek with its tail up. The old cow nudged it back out. The calf did it again, and again the cow redirected. Then the calf seemed to be teasing its mom, playing close but not in the water.

Jerry smiled as she watched the cow casually chewing her cud. The calf jumped into the creek. It lifted one leg and slipped to its side. Scrambling back onto its feet, it lifted its other back leg, and flopped down on to its face. It pushed itself back up and stopped in the middle of the muddy creek bank. With legs shaking and his head hung low, it bawled.

The old mother cow, her face showing years of experience, sauntered over to it. She licked its ear and its face, and then nudged the calf out of the mud and up the hill. The calf walked along with his head hung low and his tail between his legs.

How wonderful of God to create forgiving mothers, even in animals. Jerry bit into her apple and munched slowly. Perhaps that was what Father was doing, forgiving Corrie.

Jerry always had a good relationship with her father, but Corrie tested his patience. Corrie couldn't take his word for truth, but always had to experience everything on her own. Jerry chuckled, and smiled at the cow. "My sister is much like your calf. Do you ever get exasperated with him the way I get with my sister?"

The cow just chewed her cud and watched her from the distance. Jerry sighed and looked away. She was always confident of her father's love, but Corrie wasn't. Perhaps her father needed to go the extra mile this week to prove to Corrie his love. Perhaps Corrie needed the special treatment to help her settle down.

Jerry straightened and took a deep breath. Perhaps then, she was wrong to be upset over all Father was giving Corrie. Maybe she was

36

the one who should be held accountable. Her bad reaction to her father's love for her sister was not what God wanted from her.

She slid off the tailgate of the truck and put her lunch away. Perhaps, she needed to give them space so they could get to know each other again. After all, she had Father for the past five years. The least she could do was share him for a week or two.

Her muscles relaxed and a warm sense of purpose washed away her anger. The sun's heat seemed less fierce now. She tipped her hat to the old cow and then picked up the wire stretcher. "Thanks old friend. I think I can savvy your motherly wisdom."

The Weeds Within

Originally published in the Northview Clarion, August 1999.

"I know I can grow in this sidewalk crack,
Even though I'll lie right in her track,"
Said the seed of a weed,
Who was sure of his deed.

Then along I came
My sidewalk to claim
To pull out the weed
And improve me indeed.

But my eyes beheld the Buffalo Bean.
I felt its rare beauty must be seen.
I thought if I saw another's sidewalk
He'd have weeds too and could not talk.

So I let it be.
Don't disapprove of what you see,
For you too cannot hide, though you have tried,
The weed in your walk that I have spied.

Soap Suds on the Wall

For the child in you

Rudy Rubber Duck sat on the stool in Suzy Green's bathroom. "What a lovely day to swim in the pool outside."

Just then, a bear popped in the window.

"Oh my!" said Rudy.

"Well, hello!" said the bear. "We felt so cold, though the sun be bright, that a bath was in order. Don't mind our intrusion. A hot bath, you see, takes the chill from our bones."

"Well," Rudy said. To his surprise a second bear jumped beside the first. "I really don't think—"

"Oh look!" said the first bear. "Bubble bath!" And he began to pour it into the tub.

"No, don't do that!" cried Rudy. "That's Suzy's!"

"Turn the water on, Freddie," said the first bear to the second.

"Wait now I don't think you should—" but Rudy was too late. Freddie had turned the water on and was preparing to dive.

"One, two, three!" Splash!

"Oh no! You got bubbles and water everywhere!" cried Rudy.

"Hey, Teddy," Freddie said to the first bear. "Grab that sailboat and let's go sailing."

"Oh no, you don't!" Rudy hopped up and down on his stool in fury. "That's Suzy's sailboat!"

But Teddy jumped into the tub with the boat in his hand.

"You'll wreck it," Rudy cried. "That boat was made by Suzy's grandfather. There isn't another like it."

But the bears ignored Rudy.

"Let's make a storm!" suggested Freddie.

Teddy began to make waves in the tub. The waves grew larger and larger, and the bears laughed louder and louder, and Rudy hopped faster and faster.

Then Teddy made one big wave. The sailboat flew through the air. It flew out of the tub and landed on its side on the floor.

"Oh no!" cried Rudy. "You wrecked it. You wrecked Suzy's special sailboat. You bears are up to no good. You get out of that tub before Suzy comes in and finds you."

"Oh, Suzy won't mind," said Freddie.

"She'll not even notice," said Teddy. "Besides, it is not even broken. Lighten up, Rubber Ducky."

"Or you'll sink in the tub," laughed Freddie.

"Perhaps you are cranky because you are all dried up." Teddy taunted, as he joined in the fun.

Rudy could feel himself growing red with anger, and he shouted, "Get out! Get out right now! You troublesome bears should not be here! You only cause grief, I can see. Why just look at this room. It is a disaster. The walls are dripping. The floor is covered with bubbles. The towels are all wet, and the sailboat is sure to be wrecked. Now get out I say, get out before I squeak and Suzy comes to see what it's all about."

But the bears just laughed and continued to play in the tub full of Suzy's bubbles.

From outside came a noise and up on the windowsill a third bear appeared. Poor Rudy just groaned at the thought of the trouble three bears would make.

"Hi there, Steady Hetty Bear!" welcomed Freddie and Teddy together.

"My goodness," said Steady Hetty. "You bears had your fun. Now hurry, for down goes the sun, and Suzy will be in for her bath. You won't want to disappoint her with this mess. Quick! Grab those towels and mop up the bubbles. Pick up those toys, and oh yes, do dress."

Rudy watched with caution as Freddie and Teddy obeyed Steady Hetty's every command. To his surprise they pulled out from behind the curtains two coveralls that fit them just right.

"Now hurry, sit down," said Steady Hetty. With a quick wave at the bears, she jumped down from the sill and sat beside Freddie and Teddy next to the tub.

Rudy heard Suzy call, "Mom, I still can't find my bears!"

Her mother replied in her usual sweet voice. "They will turn up, you'll see. Now go take your bath and get ready for bed. I'll read you a story when you're done."

Suzy opened the door and gave a squeal of joy when she saw the three bears by the tub. She gave all three a hug and cried, "I found them, Mom!"

Then she grabbed Rudy and filled the tub. Rudy sighed as he floated on the water. Things turned out all right in the end. He puffed himself up and smiled as he squeaked, "Of course, I knew that they would."

Brother's Keeper

When Steven asked Brittany, my stepsister, and me to help celebrate Gord's birthday I thought, "Wow! Maybe Brittany and I will finally become friends."

We headed to Lethbridge in Steven's Jeep. Between Gord and I, we had non-stop laughter for ninety miles. We were still clowning around when we arrived at Ericksen's, the ritziest restaurant in town. I stumbled on the steps and this, I know, embarrassed Brittany.

"Better be careful, Steven, or Miss Giant will fall on you." Brittany laughed, as I grabbed Steven's arm. I joined in, but the name stung as it always did. I have my Dad's height and Grandpa's weight. I look like a big-boned, six-foot, two-hundred pound female football player.

"Finally someone my height," Steven said with a smile. He was a full six foot-five, handsome, blonde, blue-eyed, and built like Rocky.

We settled into our seats and the waiter asked for our drink order.

"I'll have a Bloody Mary," Steven said.

"I'll have a piña colada," Brittany added. Her strawberry blonde hair bounced above her shoulders when she turned to me.

I was stunned. We were all under drinking age. I knew I couldn't order an alcoholic drink, but what should I do? "A Shirley Temple, please!" I blurted out and everyone broke into laughter.

"She'll have the same as me." Brittany gave a quick look that said "You'd better not say anything."

I giggled, as I always do when I'm nervous, and then looked away as though I didn't know anything was going on. Problem was I could hear Pastor Chris's voice echoing in my head, "Drinking often leads to trouble, but drinking under age breaks the law and breaks God's heart." I revolted against what it was telling me to do.

While Pastor's statement ran through my mind like a broken record, I saw Steven's face. It had a funny look as if he knew he had missed something, but wasn't sure what.

The rest of the meal was a blur. I knew that everyone was conversing, but all I could think about was that drink. It loomed in front of me like something out of a horror movie. I couldn't drink it, but could I not drink it? After all, wouldn't it be worse to insult them, than to not say anything? I was justifying my lack of action, but I wasn't ready to admit that what I really feared was losing their friendship.

The glass sat by my plate untouched through the meal. Perhaps I could accidentally knock it over?

"Don't you like your drink?" Steven asked.

"Ah . . ." I fumbled for something to say to save face, but nothing came to mind. That's when I noticed everyone looked as if they were half-asleep.

"Don't be rude, Christy, drink up!" Brittany slurred my name. They were all drunk! Horrified, I looked at the table and saw the extra glasses. Somehow, without my noticing, they had consumed several other drinks.

"No, thank you," I replied, staring at the very empty glasses cluttering the table.

"What's the matter with you tonight? You're usually so jovial?" Steven slurred his words, and then laughed at his use of the archaic word. "Jovial Christy . . . that's what I'll call you!"

I stood up, not sure what I was going to do.

"Where you going, Jovial Christy?"

"I think it is time for us to go home."

"The night is young!" Steven said, linking arms with me. "We got a movie to see yet, right guys?"

Later, Steven motioned me into the jeep, but I hesitated. I could smell the alcohol on his breath, and it made me want to vomit. "Perhaps I should drive."

"Why?"

"Well you're . . ." What was I to say? "You're drunk," and risk insulting him?

43

"Just get in, Christy!" Brittany's annoyed tone cut through the cold air, and she put her perfectly shaped body somewhat clumsily into the front seat. Steven began to lift me in so what else could I do but take my seat?

I knew it was stupid to get into a vehicle with a drunk driver, but it was my ride home. Taxis don't take people ninety miles into the country where I live.

Guilt kept needling at me as I watched the stone buildings of downtown fly by. I glanced at the speedometer and gasped.

"What's wrong, Jovial Christy?" Steven asked, as he swerved into and out of the left lane to get around a Lexus.

"Aren't you going a little fast?" I asked while my fingers dug into the leather seat.

"Nah. They always post these speed limits too slow."

Just before the next set of lights, a Ford Escort cut in front of Steven. "Hey, you idiot!" he yelled.

When the light turned green, Steven changed lanes to get around the car. The other driver sped up. I saw the next set of lights turn red. I knew that at this speed we would never stop in time.

Steven slammed on the brakes. The jeep fishtailed.

My fingers became embedded in the seat and I heard myself saying, "Oh God, help us!"

A loud bang swung us into oncoming traffic and I saw a semi-truck crush the front of our vehicle. Later I learned the bang was a Saturn Sedan hitting the back left side of the jeep.

When everything stopped moving, I sat for a moment, trying to grasp what just happened. I felt as though I had just dropped into a movie scene after a wild ride at some carnival. A moan beside me brought me to my senses.

"Gord! Are you all right?" I fumbled in the dark to undo my seatbelt.

"Christy," he whispered painfully.

Someone opened the door, and an older man looked at me. "Are you all right?"

"I am, but my friend here is not too good, and I don't know about my sister and Steven. They seem to be unconscious."

Both Brittany and Steven were slumped against their seats with the lights of the semi in their faces. For the first time, I felt afraid. Suddenly I knew they were not unconscious. No one could be pinned like that and survive. The semi had rammed into the front seats.

"I've called an ambulance and the police." I heard the man say but I was intent on getting to Brittany.

Squeezing between the two front seats, I positioned myself to look at her face. When I saw it, I felt deathly ill. Her eyes were open and lifeless. Blood was all over her face and her hair.

I began hyperventilating and scrambled back to my seat. My head was throbbing. I remembered hitting it when the jeep fishtailed.

The man pulled me out of the jeep. "Sit here," he said, as he set me in his car.

"But Steven," I mumbled. He disappeared, and I passed out.

When I came to, I was lying in a bed in the hospital. My father was leaning over me, his hair ruffled and his face pale.

"Hi honey," Dad said as he reached across and brushed the hair from my eyes.

"How is . . ." I stopped, fearing what I might find out about Brittany and Steven.

"They both died instantly."

I started crying. If only I had made Steven let me drive, they would both be alive today.

Dad held me until I gained some control, then said, "Gord is in the hall and would like to see you. Are you up to it?"

I nodded and wiped my eyes.

When Gord came in I started apologizing.

"Why didn't you say you don't drink?" he accused and ran his stubby fingers through his curly red hair.

I stopped bumbling and looked at him. I wasn't sure whether he was angry or not.

"If you had said something Steven would never have drunk anything."

"I don't know," I replied, deflated and completely ashamed.

A scripture Pastor read once came to me. "When I say unto the wicked, Thou shalt surely die; and thou givest him not warning, nor speakest to warn the wicked from his wicked way, to save his life; the same wicked man shall die in his iniquity; but his blood will I require at thine hand."[1]

Gord sat down at the end of the bed. "It's just I know that Steven had a lot of respect for you, and if you had spoken up he would have stopped. I know I would have."

---

[1] Ezekiel 3:18

It has taken months to come to terms with the guilt and accept responsibility for my lack of action. I wasn't held accountable by a court of law, but my conscience condemned me for what I could have said.

Worrying about what they would think of me was stupid. Now I'll never have a chance to be Brittany's friend or be a better friend to Steven. Maybe Steven would have stopped drinking and maybe he wouldn't have. Regardless of what his decision may have been, I have learned that, unlike Cain in the Bible, I am my brother's keeper.

Silent Cry

Humiliation consumed Sarah as she walked past a group of whispering girls. She knew they were making fun of her—a stupid, naive freshman. Would she ever be able to leave behind her first month of high school?

The horrible night of her first party flashed through her mind. That night her destiny was set. She was played for a fool, and now she wore the brand.

The Junior Class girls had invited her to the Marina Trails for a party. They got her drunk, but that wasn't the worst. Some boys showed up and they fixed her up with Jered, a hunk from the football team. Then, like a retreating troop, they fell back and left her alone with him. Her stomach churned at the memory, and she wanted to throw up. What happened destroyed her. He left her for dirt, hooting and hollering to the other boys over his triumph. She sobbed while she tried to cover herself, swearing she would never trust anyone again.

Sarah got her books from her locker and closed its door. More catcalls and jeers were sent her way. It had been like this for six months, and it wasn't likely to change. "God, can't you please make it change?"

The bell rang as she entered her classroom. She headed to the corner in the back of the room with her arms full. There she might find some solitude.

She stumbled. Books, papers, and pens flew everywhere. Wildly, she grabbed the flag on the wall to keep from falling. Laughter and crude names filled the room.

47

Humiliated, she glanced back and realized that one of the boys had stuck out his leg to trip her. Fighting back tears, Sarah picked up her books.

As she reached for her notepad, a hand touched her fingers, and she quickly withdrew her own.

"Here, Sarah," Carol, the girl who sat behind her, said in a soft voice as she handed it to her.

Sarah nodded curtly and sank into her desk. A lump in her throat made it hard to speak. Her mind whirled with the replay of yet another embarrassing incident.

The taunts and laughter from the other students continued.

If only she could escape to a place where no one would bully her. If only someone would look beyond her past mistakes. *Oh God, why can't there be someone?*

The last bell of the day rang, and she bolted for the door, desperate to avoid the other students. Someone called her name. She kept going, not wanting to take the usual abuse that followed.

"Sarah! Stop! I want to talk with you!" Carol's voice bounced above the shouts of students and banging locker doors.

With her stomach churning, Sarah hesitated. She turned, fearing the worst, but desperately wanting to trust Carol.

"Sarah, hi," Carol said breathlessly, as she caught up to her. "I was wondering if you would be interested in coming to our youth group's hayride on Friday night. Should be a lot of fun."

Sarah studied Carol's face. Was she serious or was this just another trap to take advantage of her and make her look foolish. "Why me?"

Carol smiled. "I just thought you might like to come."

Last time Sarah went with a bunch it ended in misery. Could Carol be trusted? Sarah knew Carol didn't hang out with the Junior Class girls at school, but would she be any different? Sarah looked at her feet and fidgeted. "I might be busy. I'll check with my parents."

"Well if you can, we are meeting at the Baptist Church on Broadway, just past the old Cargill Elevator at 8:00 p.m. Here's my number if you need a ride." Carol passed Sarah a card, then said a quick "Catch ya later," as she headed across the street to her home.

Sarah stared at the card. Would she do it?

But there was no time to contemplate before some boys strutted up to her. "Yo, Sarah. want a good time?" One of the boys jeered, making a rude gesture at her. A couple of them grabbed her arms and made further rude comments.

"Let go of me!" she ordered. Their comments filled the air and gagged her mind. Her stomach rose to her throat.

A strong voice broke through the jeers. "Boys, let her go!"

Sarah kept her head down.

The man stepped between her and the boys. He wore black pants and dress shoes. Who wore shoes like that in this pigsty of a farm town? She raised her head enough to see Carol standing by the man in the suit. The boys stopped, letting go of her arm, and scurried away like frightened rats.

Carol put her arm around Sarah's shoulder. In a calm, kind voice she said, "Sarah, this is my father, Pastor Jenkins, of Turner Baptist Church."

Sarah nodded and swallowed hard. "Thank you, sir." She bit her lip; shame washed over her, but his gentle smile touched her shattered, scared heart. "It is nice to meet you."

"The pleasure is mine. Carol told me she invited you to our hayride. Why don't you come over to our house for a soda, and we'll tell you all about our plans for that night? We hope you will come."

She glanced at Carol. Perhaps she could trust Carol. Maybe she could even go to the hayride. "Sure," she replied. The churning of her stomach slowed and, for the first time in months, hope took root.

Bade Guest Good-bye

Sue found Shari's visitor disturbing. Her daughter, Shari, usually had better taste in friends. This woman, however, spoke with a refined British accent and carried herself with the poise of an aristocrat—a poise that hinted of experience beyond Sue's own forty-five years. Yet this Tamara woman could be no older than twenty. Sue needed to find a way to convince Shari this woman was no good.

Tamara had dark, peremptory eyes. She looked at Sue with such intensity that it unnerved her. She ran her finger around the edge of her teacup. Yes, she had agreed to let Tamara stay, but one look at her extravagant clothes and enormous pieces of luggage made her wonder how she could afford to keep such a guest.

"Shari should be here soon," Sue said.

Tamara looked down her long nose at her and raised one eyebrow.

Sue sighed. She recalled the day Shari told her about Tamara. Shari was so excited to meet such an intelligent woman.

"I believe Shari said you are a Junior?"

Tamara's head turned in a cool controlled manner.

Sue glanced over to the counter where Tamara had been gazing. Her Bible rested in its usual place. Did that hold Tamara's attention?"

"Yes." The woman's voice deepened.

Sue's cheek twitched. How could this . . . this creature have such a hold on her cheerleader-like daughter?

"Would you like another cup of hot apple cider?" And may God banish her from Shari's circle of friends. Sue stiffened. She shouldn't have such uncharitable thoughts.

Tamara's eyes pierced hers.

Sue set her jaw.

"Thank you."

Sue nodded and let a slow breath out as she poured Tamara another cup.

Shari bounded into the room. "Oh Tamara, I'm so glad you came." She gave the woman a quick hug. "How was the drive?"

"Droll my dear, very droll." Tamara waved her hand like the Queen of England. "I find your common American drivers quite amusing in their fruitless antics to get ahead of one another."

Sue turned away to keep Tamara from seeing her roll her eyes.

Shari giggled, "Oh I know. They so lack sophistication."

"Quite so my dear, quite so." Tamara's voice rose with an air of superiority.

"I suppose in England they are much more civilized?" Sue worked to keep the sarcasm from her voice.

"Of course darling, of course."

"Will you be staying for Christmas?" Shari asked. "I told Mother you would."

Tamara lifted her chin. "I might."

Sue lifted an eyebrow. "You could join us for our Christmas Eve service. Our choir does a lovely cantata, and this year there will be a play as well."

"How quaint." Tamara swirled her cup, and Sue squelched the desire to slap the arrogant look off the woman's face. "It should be quite amusing I'm sure."

Knowing Shari had written the play two years ago, Sue glanced at her daughter.

Shari's face twisted.

Sue had never seen such an expression on her daughter's face. She touched Shari lightly on the arm. "Are you all right?"

Shari turned worried eyes to her. "Do we have to go Mom? I mean, it's not exactly Tamara's style."

Sue raised her eyebrows. Her back stiffened. "Any guest in our house will join us for church. It hurts no one to hear the true reason we celebrate Christmas."

Tamara gave a low laugh. "No, it likely won't hurt to hear the fable."

"Fable?" Sue fought to keep her anger under control.

"Of course." Tamara's arrogant smile reeked as much as her musky perfume. "Who could possibly believe that a virgin could become pregnant. It takes two, you know."

Sue blushed and noticed her own daughter turn pale. "There is more to the story than the virgin birth. If you stop there you are only getting a small portion. The whole story includes how her baby grew to be a Man purer than anyone else. A Man who through His works demonstrated He was indeed God incarnate . . . a Man who chose to die that we might have eternal life with Him."

Tamara threw her head back and laughed. She brought her eyes down and leveled them on Sue. "Anyone who believes that is a simpleton."

Shari stiffened next to her.

Sighing, Sue put her fingers to her temple. *Lord how do I deal with this?*

"Are you calling me a simpleton, Tamara?" Shari's voice rumbled with rage.

Sue's head snapped up.

"Because if you are, let me point out to you my four A's in my four science courses, versus your four C's in your four liberal arts courses." Shari spoke in a slow, controlled voice.

Tamara waved her hand at her. "Come on Shari, you don't believe these tales do you? After all we've done together? I would never have thought that of you."

Shari looked at Sue with a pained expression.

Sue lifted the corner of her mouth in an encouraging half smile.

Shari bit her lip and looked toward the doorway that opened into the living room.

Turning in her chair, Sue followed Shari's gaze to the nativity scene that sat on the coffee table.

With a deep breath, Shari turned back to her guest. "Tamara, I went to college to learn, but I wasn't discerning. I thought I needed to learn everything so I listened to you. I went to the meetings and watched the videos, thinking that knowledge of those lies would make me more astute." She turned and her eyes bore into Tamara's. "But I never once said I did not believe in God, in Jesus, or in the Gospel."

Sue repressed the desire to jump up and kiss her daughter. Instead she folded her hands and stared at them, while a smile quivered on the corner of her lips.

"Tamara, you need to hear the truth." Shari held her voice steady, which made Sue proud.

Tamara snorted. She stood and grabbed her expensive clutch bag. "I thought you were intelligent, Shari." She picked up her faux fur wrap and flung it around her shoulders. "I don't associate with farces."

Sue all but cheered as Tamara waltzed to the door with the arrogance of a vain peacock. When the door clicked behind the woman, Sue burst into laughter. "Well done, my child. Well done." And she gave Shari the biggest, happiest hug she'd given her in years.

Mock Interviews Regarding the Proverbs 31 Woman

"This is Carol Contentious for KWCA Radio standing on the street corner of Opinion Road, and Excuses Highway to interview the notorious Proverbs 31 Woman and other passer-bys. This woman is renowned for her hard work, commitment to her family, and generous in giving to the poor and needy."

"Here she comes now. Excuse me, ma'am, could we have a minute of your time?"

"Yes? Can I help you in any way?"

"Yes, ma'am, why are you such a hard worker?"

"For the fear of the Lord. Now, can I be of assistance? If not, I must hurry home to make more linen girdles. If you please excuse me."

"There she goes, not a moment wasted of her day. Oh look, here comes a woman dressed in silk clothing and fine gold jewelry. Excuse me ma'am, would you be willing to answer a few questions for our listeners?"

"Oh my, yes. I am on my way to the World Relief Benefit. You know, I am coordinator of this fine event."

"Yes, well, ma'am, what do you think of the Proverbs 31 Woman?"

"Who? I've never heard of her. Does she run in Elite Town social circles? Otherwise I have likely not met such a person."

"Ah, no ma'am, I don't think she does."

"Well, good day then."

"Here comes another woman. She is dressed in tattered jeans with an old T-shirt that says 'You get what's comin'. Ma'am would you be willing to tell us what you think of the Proverbs 31 Woman?"

"Oh, she's just a fictional character, I am sure. No one could do all she does and remain sane."

"Well, ma'am she does exist. We just interviewed her minutes ago."

"Oh, well, surely what is written about her could not be true. No one is that perfect. I mean really. Good day, I need to see a man about a new TV. My old one broke right in the middle of my favorite soap opera."

"Good day. Here comes a lovely lady. She has three children trailing her. Ma'am, could I take a few minutes of your time to ask you your opinion of the Proverbs 31 woman? Our listeners are ready to hear your take."

"Samuel, get your thumb out of your mouth. Can't you see we are being stopped by a reporter? Clarabelle, stand up straight and fix your skirt. Susie, stop picking your nose. Excuse me; miss what is this about the Proverbs 31 woman? Oh my, if only I could have her wealth and beauty and servants. If I had all her servants and money I could do all she does too. Samuel, stop pulling on that lady's hair! I'm off to take these brats to daycare. Good day, miss."

"Our time is up folks. It appears few people find the Proverbs 31 woman believable, yet we met her today. Perhaps tomorrow we will visit the gates of our grand city and interview her husband. That's all for now folks, this is Carol Contentious reporting for KWCA radio."

HOLLYWOOD'S HORRENDOUS HALLUCINATIONS

Jejune jealousy will not make a Soap.
Jocular jeopardy attracts the sit-come pope.
But where amongst these T.V. shows
Does one assess where wild seed sows?

Lurid love scores high on the screen.
Loyal-love movies are so rarely seen.
Perhaps for clarity we should adopt Greek
Where meanings of love one needs not seek.

Vile violence lures adventurous viewers.
Venomous ventures take them to intellectual sewers.
One wonders why the world spawns villains,
And at society's loss, Hollywood makes millions.

Treacherous trails lie ahead for innocent minds
Who seek goodness and truth, and a love that binds.
Has constant bombardment of baneful scenes
Kept us from finding Truth's fruitful means?

Our

Journey

Literary Aspirations

As Explained by a Descendant of Baalam's Donkey

I wandered into the barn after hours of sitting at my desk. My spectacles sat crooked on my nose, and my mind felt like the bran mash I fed my donkeys.

"Creating is hard work," I said to myself as I sank to the pile of straw. My donkey, Marybelle, munched on hay and twitched her ears, looking at me with her wise brown eyes.

The past week endured many rewrites of a story I determined to make a literary masterpiece. Unfortunately, the battle between pen and paper stripped my mind of all creative particles. The pen sat lost on a page destined to make me a pauper in the literary world.

"Reflection is a necessary process," I said aloud, as though justifying my presence in the barn. Marybelle licked her lips in quiet agreement, and switched her tail at a fly.

I snuggled down in the straw. My mind meandered through the land of storytelling, with its mountains of enchantment and trees of profound wisdom. Perhaps, I thought to myself, I might refine my craft if I listen to the sounds of this world.

A noise came from Marybelle. At first it sounded like a nicker. I sat up. Donkey's don't nicker, they brae. I leaned forward, and to my surprise, the noise I heard was not a nicker, but a noisy whisper, "Your life experiences and your God-given imagination are your sources for creative writing."

Shocked, I cleared my throat and whispered back, "Marybelle, is that you?" Then I blinked and thought how silly, so I said, "Could you repeat what you said and perhaps, if you will, expound upon it please?" For I thought if this were a joke then the more that was spoken would reveal the one who truly spoke.

Then my donkey cleared her throat and replied, "From the depths of your memory come thoughts and emotions that will be real to those who read. Your imagination will feed the setting and plot where these feelings may be revealed. The use of life experiences and imagination enchant your readers, and they will feed upon them as food for intellect and drink them as water of moral reflection. Then your story will shape the readers' muses and perhaps cause them to challenge the way they currently view the world."

Caught up in the discussion, I forgot that it was a donkey that spoke and felt compelled to ask, "But how do I challenge the reader's worldview and perspectives on morality?"

"Through literary techniques!" She brayed and I felt the fool.

"Of course, of course," I mumbled to myself.

"A metaphor, in comparing two things, sheds light on the inexplicable. A parable, as our Lord did use, enlightens far more than an explanation ever could. An allegory teaches the way the Biblical account of Jonah and the whale is a picture of Christ's burial and resurrection." She sighed and her ears twitched. "The words and actions of your characters reveal something much deeper than typed words on the page. Your characters are alluring elements that are better known by your reader than perhaps the reader knows himself. What the characters say and do, given their plausible setting and circumstances, provoke emotions within a reader. They promote an understanding of others he may not otherwise have had."

Marybelle shifted her weight, as donkeys do, from one hind leg to the other. "Your character must be consistent, and though her personality lends itself to certain actions, a story turns when, with proper motivation, she acts upon her conflict and hence resolution is made. Naturally, these acts entail decisions made based on the character's conclusions about the circumstances in which she finds herself. Much the way you make decisions about us animals. Your personality is always present, and your conclusions are based on your limited understanding of us creatures."

Now I shifted my weight to my knees and wondered how a donkey could conclude I had limited understanding. However, before I had time to interject, Marybelle continued her monologue.

"Writing creates illusions, just as Jesus used images of something real to teach a difficult concept or a truth that appeared abnormal. For example, do you remember how He taught that it is easier for a camel to go through the eye of a needle than for a rich man to get into heaven? Well, that is an illusion. We cannot imagine a smelly, stubborn camel going through the eye of a needle, and thus His point was well made."

I thought that was the pot calling the kettle black. There were times I could not get Marybelle through a ten-foot gate, yet she was calling a camel stubborn!

"Of course a story is much bigger than that statement," she mused, oblivious to my thoughts. "A story contains much more 'showing'. A story contains a flavoring of exposition, that is, information required to understand the story; a small portion of narrative, a wonderful technique for moving a story along; and a bucketful of scenes, where people and the conflicts they face are viewed close up."

She tipped her head toward me, and her left eye stared at me. "The plot moves forward in a scene were the character experiences conflict that thwarts the achievement of her goal and leads her into disaster. A story may even contain a half-scene, which has narrative and snatches of conversation or close up action."

"Ah yes," I agreed. "The scene, the narrative, the exposition—these are wonderful illusion-making tools." I sighed. "But I must admit, I struggle some days to make a successful scene."

"You must ask yourself what is important for the reader to see. Nothing more, nothing less." Marybelle nodded her head and stomped her hoof. "Scenes will contain conflict or power shifts, or simply give the reader inductive information necessary for the development of the plot or character. All of which, of course are made alive by the character's point of view, drawing the reader to the story with his emotional reaction to every action and dilemma."

I sank back into the straw, my mind rolling over these insights. "Yes, but how can I know when my story is a literary masterpiece?" I said, getting to the crux of my situation.

Marybelle pointed her ears forward and smacked her lips. Then she shook her head. Giving a blubbery snort, she held her head high, as though listening to some far off noise. I waited, a tad bit impatient, for I knew if I got this answer perhaps I could win the battle of the pen and paper.

"A literary piece," she started as a teacher explaining a simple concept to a rather dull child, "contains well-developed characters in a plausible plot where the setting enhances the theme of the story. The conflict causes the character and the reader to contemplate life as they know it. Circumstances and decisions lead to some resolution by the character, which the reader can believe. The reader is so drawn to the character that a relationship of close, even intimate, friendship develops and this relationship lasts a lifetime. In essence, you create a plausible world, with plausible characters, and a plausible plot. The success of such a story is granted when it grips the reader, tantalizing his intellect, toying with his emotions, as he empathizes with the character, while pushing the boundaries of his worldview."

I marveled at Marybelle's exposition and found myself asking where a donkey gained such knowledge.

"From the same person you gain your creativity," she replied matter-of-factly. "From the Creator of all, the Lord Jehovah." And to show the conversation done, she turned from her stall and plodded out to join her sister in the paddock at the end of the lane.

I lowered myself back into the straw. My mind, now revitalized, began to mold and form the imaginations that before resisted framing. I reviewed the work the pen had done and designed tasks based on Marybelle's wise words. A few hours later I stretched, yawned, and straightened my spectacles. Perhaps now, with new artillery and strategies, I could take up the battle of pen and paper. My afternoon with Marybelle proved to be of greater value than gold.

The Way

The sharp rocks tore the skin off the hands of the three wanderers seeking a place of comfort and rest. Blood dripped from their hands and stained the rocks below. The crags scraped their knees and dirt wedged deep into their sores.

Silently the trio went on, each deep in his own thoughts. The bright sunlight burned their eyes and scorched their backs exposed through torn clothes. Sweat from the heat ran off them like murky water. Unbearable pain threatened to hinder their ascent, yet they moved on—all in thought, all in hope.

Charlie Hauteur, being careful not to loosen any rocks, chose the way easiest for the others. Beautrice Bitter followed carelessly, concerned only for her own body. Bartholemew Believer mumbled often, never ceasing to look ahead. All strove to attain their goal.

The sun grew hotter—an enemy burning down mercilessly on its victims. It beat their heads until they ached with flaming fever. Their skin turned to a dark, dark red. Charlie wished the day would end so the hated sun would be gone; Beautrice cursed it under her breath; and Bartholemew sent a prayer of thanks that it was sun and not snow.

Evening came and with it a cool breeze. The wanderers reached a ledge where moss formed a cushion against the hard ground. Charlie stretched out his large, weary body and sighed loudly; Beautrice flung her small self on the soft moss; and Bartholemew knelt and sang praises, grateful for the cool breeze and soft ground.

Morning came all too soon, and with it, hunger. They had no food, so the wanderers left the ledge. The pain from hunger caused them to stumble and fall. It forced them to move slowly, even though the climb leveled to a gentle hill.

At noon, intense heat drove the trio into a forest. They shivered in fear at the cold darkness that dwelt amongst the monstrous forms of vegetation. Charlie moved the group along the edge of the frightening forest.

Unable to avoid it any longer, Charlie led them deep into the woods. Their fear increased as the forest thickened and darkened. The feeling of an overwhelming evil power surrounded them, and trepidation walked with their every step. They continued on still climbing; still trying to reach their destiny.

Beatrice fell behind. She complained of fear and cold. The overpowering sensation of something awful loomed behind, and with it, the urge to look back soon over took her. "Just one look," she said, and glanced over her shoulder. All was dark; she looked ahead; all was dark. Panic grabbed her and she shouted, running wildly. Roots tripped her, and branches grabbed and scratched her already torn skin.

Exhausted and fatigued, Beatrice stopped and slumped down. Too tired to worry about all the evil and horror around her, she leaned her weary back against a tree. Every muscle in her body ached with fatigue until they quivered. Evil lurked throughout out the woods. Her weary body wilted beneath the strain of fear.

Something brushed against Beatrice's legs and began to lick her wounds. She saw the shape of small friendly dog. She smiled and accepted the animal's gentle nursing.

Beatrice's wounds felt better and she stood. The animal moved away. Following the soft steps of the animal, she found herself in a dark clearing. Weeping and gnashing of teeth could be heard and she trembled. The dog's form changed into a huge wolf and it turned on her. The heat of its breath caused her to sweat. Her throat burned, and all that was bad encircled as the wolf's teeth closed onto her small frame.

On marched the other wanderers. With an endless energy Bartholemew Believer overtook Charlie. Charlie's hope began to wither, while Bartholemew's eyes fixed on a light. It seemed to give him strength and energy, but Charlie wearied at its sight. His eyes sought relief in the ground that flowed beneath his every step.

Bartholemew spied a clearing to the right and a bit below them. People laughed and played and feasted on all sorts of foods. Sure peace and rest could be found there, he thought, but he focused again on the light. It called to him. He continued with Charlie following behind.

The forest thinned, but the trail steepened providing treacherous footing. Heat from the sun intensified and ignited fire in Charlie's blood, robbing him of strength.

They reached the tree line, and climbed among rocks. As they crawled along a cliff, Charlie slipped and fell. Bartholemew grabbed for him. Charlie slipped beyond his reach.

The air grew hotter until flames burned Charlie's body. On he fell, endlessly.

Bartholemew wept. His friends were gone; his strength was gone. His thoughts ran wild as his journey passed before him. In despair, he murmured softly and bowed humbly.

After a time, Bartholemew raised his head and again fixed his mind and eyes on the light. A warm, determined smile broke through his tears. His heart filled with hope, and his faith strengthened. Rising to his feet, he began again, singing praises.

Scrambling upward, excitement increased Bartholemew's faith and strength. As he drew closer to his destination, he became lighthearted and exhilarated. The ascent, though difficult, seemed almost pleasurable, for each step drew him nigh unto his everlasting home. Higher and higher he climbed.

Falling rocks bruised his legs. Bartholemew rubbed them and continued. Thorns and sharp stones scratched and tore at his skin and clothing. He persisted, and his mind and eyes stayed upon the light.

With rapturous glow, the light filled its kingdom. Peace and joy filled Bartholemew Believer's heart and enabled him to endure all pain and sorrow. He knew he would reach his destination. He would persevere.

Over one last boulder he trudged, and before him stood the most awesome sight he had ever seen. A radiant light shone all around. All that was of great and holy splendor and purity flooded upon him.

Awestruck, Bartholemew approached. He saw a city made of precious jewels, with pearls for gates, and streets of gold. Entering through the gate, all the dirt and pain of the journey fell off of him. Hunger and thirst no longer tortured him. He became eternally filled with peace and joy, and was greatly comforted.

Soon Bartholemew stood before the light and knew he had reached his destination. He saw creatures with six wings singing praises and thousands of others like him worshipping. Knowing he would no longer suffer and would live eternally, he lowered his head, knelt, and worshipped.

The Unseen

Cory's lips formed a delicate bond on the glass, while her blue eyes firmly fixed on the man across the table. She tipped the ornate goblet and let the juice flow into her mouth. Without blinking or looking away, she finished the drink and set the goblet down on the oak table.

The aroma of a prime rib roast still filled the room and mixed with the fragrance of white roses. These pleasant smells, however, could not thwart the tension that threatened to overcome her sensibilities.

Watching the cynical movements of the man's eyes, Cory thought herself daft to have come to this meeting. Her inquisitive nature won against her better judgment, and now she must cultivate courage to overcome the barbarous facts revealed to her.

She bit her lip. Living her life in an oasis of kindness, untouched by the obscure and obscene, she never experienced obstacles, or odious circumstances.

She folded her napkin, fully aware that he followed her every move.

As the daughter of a rich man with great integrity, evil never touched her, until now. Not that she was unaware of the perverse world outside her gated estate, but her exposure was limited to stories she heard as a child—until this horrible week.

He gave her a smirk.

Rubbing her forehead, she regretted becoming restless. A result, her tutor said, of being a teenager living in a storybook world. She pressed the heels of her hands against her eyes. Why hadn't she listened? She had suppressed those taunting feelings of curiosity until her seventeenth birthday when the desire to explore the unknown would not retreat. She succumbed and now her perfect world was sabotaged. Lowering her hands to the table, she spread her bony fingers far apart.

His upper lip curled as he gazed at them.

Shuddering, she quickly pulled them beneath the table and shot him a look of scorn. This man had ruined everything.

The man smoothed wiped the corner of his lips with his thumb and finger.

She grimaced. Why had she joined that newsgroup on the Internet? Master Gates spent many hours training her in computer programming, including web page development, but he never encouraged her to join any groups. Her submissive nature allowed his guidance to lead her opinions regarding contact with others on the World Wide Web.

"You were right to seek knowledge from groups."

Could he read her mind? She groaned. Why had she snuck into her father's den? She swallowed—it was gratifying, visiting groups and chat rooms, haphazardly opening a whole new world. But she should not have done it. Those interactive websites were so fascinating—and being able to communicate with people all over the world, she needed that. So she thought, but look where it got her. The roast beef turned to stone in her stomach.

"You've broadened your horizons, discovered new people, and now your opportunities are limitless."

Cory had enjoyed reading the discussions on various computer-related topics. The chat rooms she joined gave her new perspectives far different from her tutor's. They raised questions she never considered. But that was when she began emailing the man who now sat across from her. She closed her hands into tight fists. Their regular correspondence gave no indication of his pernicious nature. She found their on-line chats quite invigorating and cherished the more personal email he sent, but now she knew the truth.

She frowned, and her gaze fell to her lap. She never considered her father vulnerable, until now. Because of her weakness, his reputation would be jaded. This heinous man across the table dared to sell her story to the tabloids. His article described in morbid detail their first meeting. Somehow she had to convince him to retract those damaging words, but she lacked experience in confrontation. Her pleadings had only sharpened his merciless words.

"I only told the truth." He sneered.

As if his truth justified his actions. She did not know the truth before their first meeting. Her secluded life had kept it from her. Stepping from the walls of her home had made her prey to cruel creatures such as this man. The truth was injurious, not to her, but to her father who had protected her from offensive reactions.

"How long did you think you could live in those hallowed chambers before someone would find out?" he questioned in an indiscreet voice that echoed off the restaurant walls. "You're more than an invalid, Cory. You're an inferior freak of nature." He reached across the table and grabbed her arm. "Have you never looked at yourself? Can't you see that you are deformed?"

"If I am so hideous to look at"—she spurted out in a flood of tears—"Then why did you agree to see me again?"

"Because you need to understand that your father has done you no favor in keeping you hidden from the world."

Cory jerked her deformed arm away. "Your words are unbearable!" she screamed. "How dare you pretend to do me a favor when the only one benefiting from your vile article is you!"

"You are very talented and I want you to use that talent. Your ability to write programs and understand systems is amazing at your age." He looked into her eyes and lowered his voice, "I could make you great."

"What? By defaming my father and me? By describing me as a rotund girl with hideous lumps all over her body like a grotesque crocodile hide? How dare you!"

"I admit I was repulsed when I first saw you. Your email messages with descriptions of your beautiful and expensive clothing, made me think you were a beauty queen."

"You fool. You foul-mouthed fool! So your repulsion caused you to write . . . no, to vandalize my father's good name?"

"Don't you see Cory? Your father was ashamed of you all these years. If people knew of your deformities, he would never have become successful in the corporate world. He hid you from the world not to protect you, but to protect himself."

"You lie! My father loves me!"

"But he's ashamed of you."

"And all of this justifies what you have done?"

"Forget what I have done. Join me, and I will give you the freedom you have longed for. You'll earn your own money, and it will be more than your father has ever made."

"And that is supposed to make me happy?"

"The Internet provides great opportunities for people like you. You could be a hacker, greater than any one this world has known."

Cory stood from the table. She looked at him with contempt. "If you thought your article describing my father as a villainous monster would make me want to join your corrupt organization of hackers— no, thieves—you are wrong! Your email, filled with intimate words of love, were nothing more than serpent verbiage. Your article was nothing more than fabricated lies. My father is no monster and neither am I. I see now I was foolish to think a relationship could ever be formed over the Internet."

She gave him a cold and hostile look before she turned on her heel, lowered the veil to cover her ugly face, and left the restaurant. Never again would she give into those feelings of curiosity for what the world had to offer. They led to corruption and inhumanity. Her talents belonged to her father. He could take care of her; has he not always met her every need? To the world, she might look like a lumpy grotesque crocodile; but to her father, she was beautiful. Yes, she could safely work on her software programs in her heavenly home, giving to, but not being of this world.

The Throne and the City

Originally published in the Northview Clarion, April 1998 under the title "A King's Love"

The king stood in the throne room with perplexity pulling at his heart. Surrounding him, in all their finery were his knights, baring the crests of the regions in his vast kingdom. Each knight was sober in mind and silent in speech. The king must decide. The king must determine a solution, or his kingdom would fall apart.

The tall majestic ruler moved to his throne and sat down. The ache he felt for his people drained strength from his taut, lean body. Somehow, he must reach the hearts of his wayward people. Some were already on the enemy's side. If only they knew, if only they could understand the life he could give them. But they rebelled, and he had punished those who broke the laws as an example to his people.

When the warriors deserted him in battle, the king retaliated by branding them cowards. When some of the pot traders began to break his laws, the king threw them into prison. When some of the farmers refused to pay their taxes, the king forced them to labor in his fields.

To keep the kingdom from being overrun by criminals and cowards, he must punish those who broke the laws as examples so others would not dare to do the same. But now he must find some way to reconcile the people to him; some way of turning their loyalty back to him; some way of showing them how much he wanted to bless them.

The knights fidgeted with their swords. Those who just returned from a campaign in the south informed him of the condition of the hearts of these people—a condition of sorrow and anger mixed with bitterness and only a faint glimmer of hope.

Some of the people spoke of faithfulness to the king, while trading weapons with the enemy. Others were too crippled to be any help, yet their hearts, though broken, were loyal to the king. Although the entire kingdom was badly damaged by the attacks of the enemy from all sides, a greater threat loomed before the king now, the loss of the loyalty of his subjects.

Discouragement weighed heavy on the king's shoulders. His chin rested on his fist as he leaned his elbow on the arm of his throne. He stared at the marble floor and waves of sorrow for his kingdom washed over his soul.

"May I speak freely my Lord," asked one of his knights.

The king gestured for him to continue.

The knight stepped up to the throne and bowed before him. "Good king," he said in a lofty voice. "Do not be discouraged. Rally your army and send them out to show your strength to your people. Continue to enforce your laws. Punish those who have traded with the enemy. Hang them all in the city center. For you know they deserve to die."

The king groaned and waved him away. He shifted to lean on his other elbow.

"Good King," said another knight, "May I speak freely?"

The king waved him forward.

This knight also bowed before he spoke. "My Lord I suggest you burn the houses and barns of the farmers who held back their taxes. Let them see your mighty hand so that they will never again disrespect your authority. You must not give into them, or others will follow their example!"

A third knight came forward and spoke more boldly than the others. "My Lord, these men are right. If you are to hold your kingdom together you must avenge your lordship and force these ignorant people to fear the very mention of your mighty name!" He jerked his sword from its sheath in a proud salute to the king.

But the king grew angry. He slammed his fist down on the arm of his throne and thunder, "Enough!"

Rising to his feet he shouted, "Enough you knights! Have I not tried your ways and have they not failed?"

He paced back and forth in front of his throne. "Do these people love me anymore by my efforts to enforce the laws of our land? What

71

have I gained by these things? They know who I am by the fear they feel, that is all."His voice vibrated through the room while he slumped back onto his throne.

The room grew deathly quiet. Even the wind outside stopped its roar, and the birds stopped their singing. Not a sound could be heard in that great room where laws were passed and decrees were set forth.

After moments of silence, a warmth grew within the king that calmed his fears and captivated his anger. It brought with it peace and tenderness. He spoke in a gentler voice. "Does a mother not cradle in her arms a child that just fell? Does a father not forgive a son for making a mistake? Am I not also capable of these acts of compassion?"

The king sat straight in his throne. He could not keep the smile from his face that sprang forth from the joy beginning to bubble in his heart. "Tomorrow, instead of a hanging in this hallowed city, I will walk out among the people, and we will feed the hungry! From my own hand, I will feed them. We will treat the sick and the injured, and build homes for the poor. I will forgive the debts of the farmers and return them to their farms. We will rebuild this kingdom."

He stood with great majesty and held his scepter high in his right hand. "We will rebuild this kingdom not by fear, but by compassion! We will restore the pride of our people and give of ourselves to make them all become what they are capable of being!"

The knights were skeptical and felt such acts were not becoming of the king, but the next day the mighty ruler kept his word. He shed his kingly garments and wore the clothes of a common man. He fed the hungry, released the prisoners, healed the sick and injured, and built homes for the poor. He forgave his people their debts and their wrongs done against him and his mighty kingdom.

The knights were astounded with the results. The farmers returned to their land and produced ten times as much food as they did before, cheerfully paying their taxes. The pot traders stopped trading weapons and returned to trading wares in honesty. The confidence of the people was restored and their loyalty, mixed with love for the king, ran deep. The kingdom became mightier than ever before, striking fear into the heart of its enemy, all because the king, overwhelmed by love and compassion for his people, humbled himself and became one of them.

Where is the Light?

Wandering in the tunnel of darkness, a young man finds himself alone. He is lost, confused, and scared. All around him are voices and forms, but none seem friendly or interested in him. He shivers, and looks ahead.

A small light, like a star or a streetlight is in the distance. It calls him. He moves toward it. *What is it?* He continues on, slowly and cautiously; his eyes fix on this light.

A shadow crosses in front of him. He questions the light's existence. Confusion overtakes his mind, yet curiosity drives him on through the shadow toward the light.

Another tunnel appears, jutting out from his present course. Intersted, he goes into it. Cautiously he feels for the wall and follows it.

The wall is rough and the tunnel is dark. Fear grips his body and shakes it. There is no light, no way of knowing where he is going, no assurance that he will survive. He shudders. What might happen to him? He is lost.

Continuing on, for there is no place else to go, he takes one step at a time. He can hear voices again, but cannot understand them. He becomes confused and angry. What is happening?

A corner. Is this a dead end? His hands feel around the wall. He turns and looks up. The light—it is ahead of him again.

His curiosity again drives him on toward the light. Quietly, with every muscle tense, he moves.

"The light does not flicker," he speaks into the dark. "It must not be a candle. Could it be something more powerful?" His mind is in a whirl. *What is this light?*

As he continues, he stumbles many times. His knees become bruised and his jeans are torn. He falls and lands on something sharp and painful. Cautiously he picks himself up and wipes himself off. His hands feel warm and wet. They are bleeding. He winces and begins to weep. "What kind of life is this?"

He looks up and sees two lights. There is the one he saw before, and now a new one that is closer and flickers. He walks toward it. It seems to be beckoning him, telling him to follow it. He is captivated by the light's dance. He moves closer to it and hears friendly voices.

From the corner of his eye he sees the first light glowing steadily, but his attention is drawn away from it to this new light. This wavering light takes control of his mind. He walks as man in a trance, lost to outward attractions.

He moves closer until he reaches this strange light. He sees people busy in activities he does not fathom. Another step and suddenly he is surrounded by smiling faces that encircle him, talking so fast he cannot understand what they are saying. They push him forward.

His eyes widen with amazement as he sees people dressed in dull white robes scrubbing walls that are already white and shiny. Others are kneeling in front of a painting of a man. They rock back and forth, mumbling and wailing. He is pushed again.

In front of him steps a man dressed also in a dull white robe, but his face is red, not pale like the others. His voice is otherworldly, seeming to echo yet low and soft. Intrigued, the young man follows this robed person.

The robed man says something in a language the young man cannot understand, and he shoves a scrub brush in his hand. The young man sees others scrubbing the floor. *Strange,* he thinks as he looks about him, while rolling the brush in his hand.

Before long, the young man kneels beside the others. His hand moves back and forth; his back sweats profusely and his arms are fatigued.

As time passes, his work dulls his mind. He is no longer aware of what moves around him, nor of what he is doing. His eyes become sore and tired, and he longs for sleep.

A steady chanting fills the room; a constant drilling of words into his mind.

74

The young man takes up the chant, moving his brush to the beat, driven by the cadence.

A tap on the shoulder.

He looks up. Pains shoots through his body.

The man with the red face and white robe beckons him with a long crooked index finger that has a claw-like nail.

The young man rises. His muscles are stiff and his legs are numb. His ankles burn as blood rushes to them. His head nods heavily. His thoughts swirl around him like flies around a sweet drink.

The robed man takes him into another room. Faces surround him; teeth chatter; tongues move; eyes stare.

Where am I?

People push him forward, their gaze boring into his eyes.

His heart races.

Everything revolves around him—faces, voices, hands.

He spins until he stumbles. "What is going on? Stop it! Stop it!" He shouts, but no one listens.

He is pushed further. People shove books and pamphlets into his hands. They offer Flowers to him for a price. The robed man continues to beckon him.

He follows.

The robed man's face turns a deeper red. His eyes snap and grow larger and darker. He continues to call the young man. The young man watches with fascination. The man's robe is turning black, as black as blindness.

The young man pulls at his collar.

The air is hot and stuffy. Strange noises float around him. Screams and wails and shrieks of agony slam against his ears.

Everything is getting darker.

Red flames laugh and dance a war dance.

The young man stands in a pool of his own sweat. His blood races through his body.

His eyes fix on the robed man, who is no longer a man but a beast. The creature has many horns and eyes. Eyes that pierce; diabolic eyes stealing his very soul.

"Run!" the young man screams.

His legs only bring him closer to the beast and the fiery pit ahead.

"I must get away!" His efforts are futile. *A light! A light is to the right! Turn to it! Get away!*

The young man struggles against the force that holds him. The beast's eyes fix on him.

Got to get away. Head for the light, Now! His mind screams at him.

He breaks away. With fear driving him, he runs to the light. *Got to get away!* Breath is squeezed from him. He stumbles. He stops.

Lonely and deserted. His body trembles, and his mind becomes a whirlpool of fear and confusion. He begins to cry.

Looking up, he sees the light is closer, shining bright and warm. A soft, gentle voice whispers from the distance. A sense of peace and calm draws him.

He steps toward the light. Guilt covers him. Grief sends torrents of tears down his cheeks. Anguish bends him and presses him down to his hands and knees. Fatigue consumes him.

Crawling toward the light, he lifts his head enough to call for its source to help him.

Energy pulses through him as the source pulls him to his feet.

Excited, he races and falls before the bright cross from which the source shines. His soul fills with gathering clouds of sorrow and he repents of all his iniquities.

The Light from the cross surrounds him, lifts him up, and becomes a part of him. It burns away his sin, leaving him with peace and joy. He is freed from worries.

His body changes and he finds rest from all previous trials and burdens.

Exuberance and gladness, and everlasting joy fill his heart, soul, and mind. The young man has found all that he needs.

A spirit of faith and love preside with him forever.

Alice Egord and Lily White

Nethertheless I have somewhat against thee, because thou has left thy first love. Remember therefore from whence thou are fallen, and repent, and do the first works; or else I will come unto thee quickly, and will remove thy candlestick out of his place, except thou repent.

Revelations 2:4-5

"We have reached five billion dollars through our 'Save Our Planet' Campaign." Alice Egord watched herself say on television to Tiffany Wicks, the internationally acclaimed journalist for the All World Network. "The people of this planet have rallied around this campaign in agreement. Our planet is in a crisis situation with Global Warming."

Thrilled by her perfect appearance and speech, Alice smiled. The interview went well and seemed to silence any opposition from those nasty right wing fundamentalists. She was making roads into every area of their nation. Every group, every corporation, and every organization will soon be toting the "Go Green" line. Yes, her work was beginning to pay off.

"Ma'am, would you like to inspect the organic fruit and vegetable platters for the reception?" Her efficient assistant, Starr, directed her to the long line of tables featuring organic produce from around the world.

Her skin tingled at the purity of the display. Not a single plastic plate. Not one piece of fruit or vegetable grown by or with chemicals. She sighed. A more perfect picture of a unified world there could never be.

Alice walked along the tables, feeling the rising energy of success. This reception would be a grand show of solidarity, and what better place to have it than in her newly converted "Green" mansion?

"Ma'am, would you like to see the display tables? There is one here from every group you met with this past year."

This was so exciting. She loved the idea of giving the campaign supporters promotional tables to keep them on board and motivated to give.

Her wood sandals pressed the green lawn beneath them, sending up the clean fragrance of freshly cut grass—cut by a manual mower, of course. A perfect scent for this feast to remember their success in their work to save Mother Earth.

"I thought you would be especially interested in this one from the Coalition of Baptists." Starr's hand stroked the wool tablecloth on which the display rested. "I love this title, *A New Baptist Covenant*."

Alice's heart bounced. This truly was a victory. "It's about time these people realized the fate of the world. It is good to see that they have their priorities straight now."

Starr touched Alice's arm. "I see some of our guests are arriving. Is that not the president of the Evangelical Committee?"

Barely containing the energy building inside her, Alice bobbed on her toes. "Yes, and I believe he has persuaded his committee to call Global Warming an issue of utmost importance." Alice leaned close to Starr's ear. "He told me in confidence that he plans to convince them to channel some of the moneys dedicated to missions to our 'Save Our Planet' Campaign. After all, if the world is no longer livable, then there will be no one to preach their gospel to."

Alice squeezed Starr's hand, and then hurried along the stone edge that lined the natural pond. Her foot slipped. She screamed and tumbled down. As her head struck a rock, sharp pain shot through her skull, and she slipped away into a black abyss.

#

Lily's frail hands shook as she slid the check into the envelope. This was the last one she would write to her son, Billy. She was so proud of him and his missionary work in the Fiji Islands.

She coughed and licked the seal. "Dear Lord, let them use this wisely. Draw the Fiji people to you. Open their ears that they may hear Your wonderful Gospel."

The obnoxious roar of a motorcycle interrupted her prayer.

She looked out her window and saw the machine fly up to the Egord Mansion. A fancy Ford Escape Hybrid those environmentalists were always driving followed the motorcycle. A stream of other hybrids raced by as well.

Lily sighed. "Alice Egord must be having another one of her receptions."

She placed a stamp on the envelope and set the envelope on the shelf by her door. Pastor would be by later to pick it up and to drop off Wednesday night's prayer list. Her lower lip sagged. Few people came to visit her anymore, but at least she could pray for them. There was Johnny, the Youth Pastor, and his wife. Such kind people. And then Mrs. Hanover's operation . . . when was that? Tomorrow, perhaps. She must remember to pray for that.

A great pressure around her chest caused her to stumble and grasp the back of her couch. These pains were coming more frequently now. She breathed deeply, taking in the musty smell of her fifty year old couch, which was one of the few things she and her husband bought new. Its smell was crisp and clean and pleasant then. Carefully she moved around to the front of it and slumped onto the cushions.

Her hand still clutched her checkbook. She took a deep, painful breath and smiled. One check left. She would make it out to her church. "Let's see, Billy's was one hundred. That leaves two hundred for the church, the last of my money." She carefully wrote the numbers on the lines and signed it.

Shivering, she wiped beads of sweat off her forehead before dropping this last check into an offering envelope. Nausea bent her as though punching her in the stomach. Not long now and she would see the beloved face of her Savior. Taking a ragged breath, she smiled. Warmth surrounded her as a sharp pain stabbed her chest. She gagged for air but rejoiced when none came.

Soon and Very Soon. The chorus rang through her mind as she rose above her small trailer, above the quarter acre she called home. A soft white light surrounded her and the pain disappeared; her youth restored; a new robe alighted her shoulders. She beheld her mansion on high.

#

Something hot and sharp poked Alice. Her eyes fluttered opened as she breathed in smoke and gagged. She waved her hands before her face. Had she fallen into a furnace?

Someone cackled behind her, and she whipped around. Fears and sorrows pressed down upon her with hands as real and weighty as that of a body builder. Pain licked every one of her nerves as the voice cachinnated again.

"Well done my good and faithful servant. You enticed those ugly Baptists away from spreading the Gospel. You fed the Evangelicals with lies that turned their backs on missions. You led the blind away from God's plan of salvation to surround themselves with the fears of a dying creation, fooling them into believing they could do something." The voice snorted. "As if they were the Creator, God."

Shivers went down her spine, despite the intense heat. Where was she? Was this just a bad dream? Would she wake up soon?

Hot breath singed her cheeks as the voice spoke again. "You empowered them to put before the enemy another god, the god of Mother Earth. Now damnation is inevitable. Well done, I say, well done."

Alice moaned and it echoed around her, mixing with the tortured voices of a million others. This was not how she planned eternity.

Lily jumped up and her cheeks stretched with a grin. "Matthew! My dear brother."

"Oh sister, thank you for telling me about Jesus when I was merely a boy."

More people circled her.

She marveled at the unfamiliar faces that seemed so glad to see her.

"Yes. Lily, thank you for sending the money to our missionary in Sri Lanka." A thousand voices greeted her. "Because of your faithful giving, we are here with our wonderful Lord and Savior."

Her chest rose with joy. Could this be true? Did her small gifts really bring this many people the message of God's redeeming love?

Another woman embraced her. Lily immediately recognized the spirit of this dear person. "Katya!" Lily jigged up and down on her tip toes. "What a joy to see you!"

"Dear Lily, if it wasn't for your patient, persistent witness I would not be here. Thank you!"

"Lily."

She knew that voice. It filled her with warmth from the top of her head to the tips of her toes. Every part of her tingled with joy, and she turned. Biting both her lips, she could hardly contain her excitement. She had spent sixty years of her life waiting for this moment when she could look into this face of light.

"What a blessing it is to have you with Me in Heaven, my precious saint and faithful servant."

She ran into His arms and basked in His beautiful presence for eternity.

A Ride to Remember

Three pogo stick-like leaps into the air and I knew I was in trouble.

With a yank of the rein and a kick from my legs,
I tried to get that horse-turned-bronc's head out from between his forelegs.

Action was required and I needed to think quick.
Three penners in the ring,
Along with some calves, which made it quite slick.
Riders on the east fence;
A vaulting team to the west;
Grandstands stood to the south;
And on the north, guests viewed my best.

A quick survey of the land and I thought to myself,
I'd better place my landing spot bid
Before that bay bronc did.

I let out a yell (that was more like a scream)
I wanted attention, or so it would seem.
Another leap and a buck and I felt myself lurch.
We were at the east fence, where some riders did perch.
It was now or never, I thought to myself.
Another buck from that bronc and I feared for my health.
I curled my head to my stomach,
Pulled my knees to my chest,

And my arms wrapped around me while I prayed for the best.
I felt a knock to my side followed by another
As the bay's body just seemed to hover.

Before I knew it, someone was at my side.
He said, "Be still!"
But I heard those horse's feet pounding and I felt a great chill.
I mumbled, "I need to get out of this ring."
While I struggled to stand, and was up on one knee,
I saw that bay bronc aiming straight for me.

An angel of God stretched out her arm
And grabbed that bay's bridle before he caused me more harm.
I praise the Lord I'm alive today
For I could feel the breath of that big awful bay.

What a show I put on!
The response was phenomenal.

No one expected the horse to give me that ride.
I was told he was quiet and I'm not sure but they lied.

What lessons were learned?
Well my family say none,
For I'm back to training and riding for fun.
However, I beg to differ, you see,
And I'm off to buy a safety vest,
What a joy this will be!
My ribs are broke and it's the second time.
To break them again would only prove what a fool I'm.
No one knows what caused the bay to go bronc.
He was new to us all, you see.

He's going fine now, quiet as ever,
But no horse is predictable, as you may perceive.
It's a risk every rider takes,
Though some won't admit it,
At least not 'til some horse gives them their leave.
The best we can do is be as safe as we can.
For me, that's a helmet and a vest at hand.

Prairie

Golden stubble hair, white snow dress
Beauty stretching beyond man's vision

Soft curves faintly seen
But those who venture beyond silver road necklaces know
her sensual figure

Moods of hot and cold
Switch as easily as the wind.

She's known for harshness. Few see her grace.
Feisty in summer; bold in winter.
Spring reveals new birth.
In fall, she generously gives.

Golden stubble hair, white snow dress
Her beauty lies beneath endless blue skies.

My Mind is the Wind

My Mind is the wind
Bringing tremendous storms of passion
That drives my life in an unruly fashion.

My mind is the wind
It cools the summer heat of pain
Bringing tears, like soothing rain.

My mind is the wind
It brings the Chinook that warms the fear
And wipes away the sorrow-filled tear.

My mind is the wind.

Fall

Fabulous
Autumn
Leaves
Linger

Peanut Butter and Jam Sandwiches

Brown cream smoothed over silky white bread.
Red jam, sticky, glues itself to brown cream under the cover of silky white
bread.
Mouth stuck. Throat closed. Words cannot be spoken.
Milk washes.
Brown cream loosens.
Words are spoken.
Peanut butter and jam sandwiches.

This ditty comes from something I say to my kids when they are stuck for words. When they pause, I chime in with "Peanut Butter and Jam Sandwiches?" And magically, their stuck mouths give way to laughter.

A's Abiding Adventure

'**A**' acted abandoned.

'**A**'s address was absent.

'**A**' felt quite alone.

Absorbed in thought, '**A**' walked past his **a**bode in front of 'pple and 'lligator, and 'lice.

'**A**' ambled sadly until he bumped into 'llan.

'llan laughed and said, "Thank you '**A**'. Now I can be **A**llan and not be lonely any more."

'**A**' smiled and said, "You mean I do have a place?"

"Yes," **A**llan said, "In front of my name, and **A**lice's, and in front of **a**pple, **a**lligator, and of course **a**ngel."

"You also **a**bide in front of **a**pricot, **A**pril and let's not forget **a**pron and **a**ble," **A**llan added. "You **a**re **a**n important letter '**A**'."

"Really?" '**A**' replied, **a**stonished to hear it.

"**A**bsolutely!" **A**llan said. "You **a**re needed in front of **a**ardvark, **A**dam, **a**dder, and **a**lmond. Without you, we wouldn't be **a**ble to spell **a**irplanes, **a**mbulances, **a**nts and **a**stronauts. And I wouldn't be able to spell my name!" laughed **A**llan.

'**A**' laughed too. He was not **a**bandoned **a**fter all. He did **a**dd to life.

'**A**' picked up his pace and chose to have **a**n **a**biding **a**dventure finding words that begin with him.

First Day of School
A Family Anecdote

Dressed in a new uniform and shiny black shoes, the eldest daughter leaps from the van into a long awaited adventure—the first day of school. She shouts over her shoulder, "See ya later, Mom!" Apparently I wasn't needed to help her make the transition from home life to school life.

The other two kids and I return home.

We pulled into the driveway and my son says, "Mom, we forgot my sister."

I smile and reply, "She is at school today honey. We will pick her up after nap time this afternoon."

Son scratches his head and rubs his nose, then stares out the window. "But who will I play with?"

"You can play with your little sister and me."

His little sister wiggles in the car seat in front of him as he asks, "Is she here?"

Fast forward two years and my son's first day of school; we pull up to the drop off gate. "Are you ready son?"

He begins to shake his head but his older sister pushes past him and says, "Come on, let's go!" He follows, riding on the tail of her enthusiasm.

I shake the urge to cry and put a brave smile on my face for my youngest daughter. "So, shall we go home?"

"Oh yes, we can color and read stories and do things together." She did not miss her brother or sister at all.

Just for Fun

A mother stepped into her three year old's room and stopped dead in her tracks. Before her lay the contents of the dresser drawers strewn across the floor. Her daughter stood beside her with a happy smile on her face.

The mother asked, "Did you put these clothes on the floor?"

"No, Mama," the little girl said, clasping her hands behind her back and smiling sweetly.

"Did your sister do this?"

"No, Mama," answered the little girl, now holding the corner of her dress and swinging it as she twirled.

"Then how did this happen?"

"Oh Mama, they just flew through the air and landed there," answered the little girl as she giggled and twirled and skipped from the room.

Hockey and Tea Parties

A fierce game of floor hockey occupied the hall in our house. The soft puck flew down the hall to one goal and back up the hall to the other. Hockey sticks slapped and slashed. Cheers echoed through the house as a player made a goal. Stuffed animals in the bleachers (stools at the doorways of bedrooms) raised a victory cry.

"Another game! Another game!" Shouts arise, and soon the puck is dropped at center "ice" and the thunder of children's feet filled the "stadium".

"He shoots! He scores!" the announcer exclaimed from the end of the hall, and the players tumbled on the floor, rolling with laughter.

One clever Teddy Bear, with the help of Mom, carried a tray. A teapot with a pitcher of milk and a canister of sugar cubes graced the top of the tray next to a plate of Biscoff, Tea Biscuits, Ginger Thins, and the ever faithful Pure Butter Shortbread.

At "center ice" players lay down their sticks, picked up their teacups, and dressed their tea with milk and sugar. Then, with the eloquence of fine ladies and gentlemen, offered each other the delicacies of a proper childhood tea party. Of course, the stuffed animals joined in, discussing the finer points of the game.

What better way to spend a stormy day, and what better way to celebrate victory than a tea party with Teddy and friends.

Family Fun

A mother gives her four year old daughter ten pennies. "Now honey, one penny is for God. Put it in the offering plate and He will one day bless you with more."

The daughter willingly puts her penny into the plate and passes it on. After a moment she turns to her mother and says, "Mom, can you give me more so God will bless me?"

Governator's Protégé

This was written while Arnold Schwarzenegger was Governor of California

While having a tea party with his mother and his little sister, a four year old California boy asked "Will this cheese make me strong?"

The mother smiled and said, "Yes, it will."

The little boy picked up the slice of cheese and studied it for a minute. "Big and strong muscles like our governor?"

On Motherhood

Something I have noticed about motherhood is that the rules of engagement continually change. As each child ambushes you with a new stage of life, your battle strategy changes, and society (a mother's major adversary) has a whole new set of rules by which it feels you must follow.

Childhood Play

Imaginative play is the child's critical thinking

My friends and I idolized Nancy Drew. We read her books with ferocious appetites and spent our Saturdays hunting down criminals residing at the Old Place, an abandoned farm down the road from my home. Mimicking this famous girl detective's great sleuthing skills, we followed clue after clue, chasing imaginary ghosts and legendary thieves. We found birds, mice, and skunks haunted the buildings and lurked behind Caragana trees; yet critters of the human sort eluded us.

Writing messages on the walls of the old chicken coop, we waited for proof that someone else did frequent the farm. To our surprise and our elation, our messages were answered! After a little more detective work, we discovered the evil culprits—my older sister and her friends. These times shaped our social skills and developed our perspective of the world as we traversed the thin line between fantasy and reality.

Family and the Dodge Caravan

The new Dodge Caravan is proclaimed to be the best family vehicle ever, but from the way it is described I'd say its anti-family.

In *Better Homes and Gardens,* the February 2008 edition, a two page advertisement for the 2008 Dodge Caravan appears. I scanned the pictures, oohing and ahhing over the wonderful features. It comes fully loaded with *MYGIG Multimedia Systems*, halo/led lighting, and Exclusive *Sirius Backseat TV* and Dual DVDs. Imagine the possibilities!

Then I read this statement: "Nothing connects your family like the All-New Dodge Grand-Caravan."[2] I scanned the page again. Scratched my head, and thought "Okay, what exactly is it connecting my family to?"

I read on. "With available features such as dual DVDs and *Sirius Backseat TV*, it's a multiplex on wheels. Plug in your *iPod* or rock out to your stored MP3s. Either way, we put it together for you to bring your family together."

Hmmm. Picture this. All five of us are crammed into one vehicle. My husband is watching a sitcom on his *iPod*. My youngest daughter is watching *Disney Channel* on the *Sirius Backseat TV*. My eldest daughter is watching *Anne of Green Gables* on the DVD player. My son is reading a book under the halo/led lighting. Me, I'm driving, listening to some tunes on the MP3 player.

We arrive at our destination, and the people we meet ask us, "So what did you talk about on the way here?"

I stumble around, and finally blurt out. "Nothing!"

---

[2] "Dodge Caravan," Advertisement, *Better Homes and Gardens* vol. 86, no. 2 (February 2008).

"Oh." They look away. "Sooo, did you see the new bridge being built? It's spectacular."

"I saw that, did you kids?"

"No." They all say in unison.

"Sooo." Our friends shuffle their feet under the table as they tap their fingers together. "How are the kids doing in school?"

"I don't know. I haven't talked to them in so long. We've been busy you know . . . soccer, volleyball—oh and don't foget the football games we've watched every night for however many weeks. Life just gets away on us you know. I'm so glad to get away from the hectic life back home. Thank you for inviting us up for a visit."

"Sure. Say, the hockey game's on right now, why don't we turn it on."

"Sounds great."

Meanwhile, my youngest daughter found a lovely patch of poison oak in their backyard and is rolling in it. My eldest daughter is pouring her heart out to their eldest daughter about the bullies at school. My son is in the garage with their son experimenting with some chemicals they found, like the mad scientist in the book he was reading in the 2008 Dodge Caravan.

Yup. The All-New Dodge Grand Caravan sure pulls us closer together. Think I'll rush right out and buy one.

Look for the Good in Them

My daughter forgot her backpack at home so I made the forty minute round trip again, costing roughly ten dollars in gas. My son decided to be a commando and jump on an end table. The result: one broken end table. Before me stood a three year old with frustration rising from her feet and exploding out her mouth with a wail so loud Eskimos in Alaska could hear it. The dog vomited on my husband's rug, after destroying two other rugs when the contents of his bowels exploded. Out you go, dog. Who fed him the chocolate bunny anyway?

Some days I wonder if my vocabulary goes beyond: "don't touch;" "please be quiet;" "put that down;" "why'd you do that?" "Be nice to your sister;" "Stop!" "Pardon me? What did you just say?" And the full names of my children.

The life of a mother can have its excitement and its exasperation. There are days when I make a break for my bedroom, fall on my knees, and beg God to remove the pent up emotions before I look at another cherub face (though I may not be thinking the faces are so terribly angelic at the time), for I fear the cannon of irrational emotions will blow. Seeking the Lord for patience and perspective, it is on my knees that I find relief and a change of heart.

Moments later, I'll find a sweet note from my eldest daughter expressing her love for me. My son will come running up, wrap his arms around my legs and say, "You're the best mommy." My youngest daughter will bury her face in my lap, weep an ocean of tears and sob out, "I'm sorry I threw a temper."

Then the light shines, and I find God showing me the good in them, like the reverend in *Pollyanna*. I discover that my eldest is ever thoughtful and sensitive to doing God's will. Poured out on me is an endless supply of joy and energy from my son. And greeting me every hour of the day is the sweet, humble yet strong spirit of my youngest, blossoming with beauty and grace.

Each day brings its trials, but when I do what the Lord commands and turn my thoughts onto what is true, honest, just, pure, lovely, of good report, virtuous and praiseworthy (Phil. 4:8), I find even ruined rugs, broken tables, and temper tantrums can be forgiven.

Fool Them All?

Did you ever notice how people look?

We all tend to judge a person by his appearance, even if it is a subconscious assessment. Not always do we do so accurately.

Step into the local coffee shop and see what you find. You may be surprised how much your impressions of its patrons depend on how they look even without speaking to them.

Observe the lady sitting at the table beside you. She is roughly fifty years old. Her hair is pulled back in a ponytail with neat curls swirling around the back of her head. She has taken the time, you surmise, to fix her hair. Yet, you note, she is not wearing make up. The orange of her tank sweater and the musty green of her suit jacket and pants, on the other hand, indicate she knows what colors match her own natural autumn complexion and hazel eyes.

Earrings dangle from her ears, matching the simple necklace lying elegantly against her sweater. A simple ring set sits like a permanent fixture on her left ring finger. A watch of no distinction ticks time away on her refined wrist. You decide she is not wealthy, just middle class.

A scowl rests on her face, not forced, but etched enough into the lines of her face to indicate it is a regular feature. She fiddles with her keys. She swishes her coffee, apparently impatient for someone to arrive.

Her leather briefcase, black leather shoes, and a book on business management suggest she is here on business. Is she an executive? Not likely, you determine. The lack of make-up suggests this. Yet dressed as she is, you determine she is a business person—perhaps self-made.

The lady frowns, stands up, and gathers her things. With the sharp clip clop of solid yet stylish shoes she leaves the shop on what you decide is a mission to call down the one who failed to meet her.

Just before the door closes, you see her step into a Porsche. So, maybe you were wrong about the middle class assessment.

In walk two young ladies. The red head says, "did you see that lady getting into the Porsche?"

"Yeah," replies the blonde.

"Mom says she's the wife of the richest man in our city. Apparently she was a movie star ten years ago."

Oops, you realize that you were wrong.

Further study of the coffee shop attendees reveal what you believe are two businessmen—a young upstart computer guy trying to make it in the dog-eat-dog world, and possibly a couple of executives, loaded down with electronic gadgets and dressed in designer suits.

Is your assessment correct? Dare you walk up and ask these complete strangers if your thoughts were errorless?

In walks a woman, roughly forty years of age. She wears a simple solitaire ring with a wedding band. Her hair is pulled back in a ponytail with loose tendrils puffing around her head, suggesting the wind pulled them out. Her face is clean and without blemish. She wears no make-up. A leather jacket hangs from her shoulders, covering what looks to be a plain white t-shirt. She wears faded green jeans. Tall and long-legged, she walks as one having just come off a horse.

Wrinkles about her eyes suggest stress, but her face is not taut. She orders her cafe latté and sits down with her notebook. *What does she do*, you wonder. She obviously does not work in an office. Probably a mother, certainly married, could she be a simple housewife? Perhaps. She writes in her book, sips her coffee, and seems engrossed in her own world.

What is your impression? What do you hypothesize is her attitude, her life, her belief structure? I will leave that up to you. So much can be said about a person by their appearance, but I ask you, how much of it is truly accurate? Be careful now, that last person was me!

A Brave Woman Helps a Soul

Sixteen year old Lawrence Malone staggered to the bench on the back side of the grand oak tree in Baker's Park. *No one cares what happens to me.* He slumped down, and the bench creaked beneath his heavy weight.

"Careful!" a soprano voice cranked. "I nearly stuck this nail file into my cuticle!"

He glanced up and nodded an apology, then looked away. The woman, he noted, dressed like his mom. Her tight t-shirt did not cover her navel and swooped too low at the top. And her short skirt, *agh*, revealed more than he dare want to see.

A familiar lump rose in his throat; the one that came whenever his mom found a new boyfriend and she dressed like that. Lawrence pulled at his black turtleneck as though doing so would dislodge the lump.

Laughter crackled through the still air, and it echoed against the hill behind him.

He lifted his gaze to watch a mother, holding a little girl on her lap, go down a circle slide. His lump turned into an ache. When was the last time he laughed with his mom?

The mother climbed up the swinging bridge after the little girl. Squealing with excitement, the little girl clung to her mother's loose fitting jeans as they rocked the bridge back and forth.

She giggled, but he frowned. His mom would have made him stand alone. A low moan pressed out through his lips as a fear-filled memory flashed across his mind.

100

"Jimmy! Pull up your pants." the soprano screeched at a boy bent over to play in the sand. She picked up a can of soda and gulped greedily.

"Mom, can I have a drink?" asked the boy.

"No. I finished it off."

"But Mom, I'm thirsty."

"Go play in the sand. I'll get you a drink on the way home."

"But that was my soda," the boy whined.

"Yeah, but it was my money that bought it. Now go play so I can finish my nails."

Lawrence cringed at the distain in the woman's voice. Those words were reminiscent of conversations from his past. His mom hated him. He was certain of that fact.

A cry and a whimper called Lawrence's attention back to the playground. The little girl sat on the ground, holding her elbow. Her mother picked her up and cooed softly.

Pain rose behind Lawrence's eyes. Oh how he longed for such tenderness.

He lifted his shirt and pulled out the knife he tucked into his belt earlier that day. It was his father's hunting knife. Last time he visited his father he borrowed it. Today he would use it. He pulled the blade from its sheath and turned it in his hand, watching the sunlight bounce off the blade.

His stomach churned and he grew cold.

A hand touched Lawrence's shoulder. He started and glanced up. The nice mother's round face smiled down at him. The corner of her eyes turned down, as though she were sad. "Would you like some juice?" she asked as she punched a straw in a box.

"Thank you," He took the box, though nauseous.

"My name is Joanne. What is your name?"

"Lawrence."

"Nice to meet you, Lawrence." Joanne pulled out a sandwich from her backpack. She offered Lawrence half.

He took it and mumbled a thanks. If he left would she think him rude?

"That is a fine hunting knife you have."

Lawrence nodded. He didn't look at her. He couldn't. He didn't want her to guess what he had planned for that knife.

"I once had a knife like that. I stole it from my father."

Lawrence began to tremble.

101

"Then someone told me about Jesus." Joanne peeled an apple with a paring knife she drew from her backpack. She offered it to Lawrence, but this time he shook his head. After taking a bite, she asked, "Do you know about Jesus?"

Lawrence shook his head. A flood of weakness gushed over him.

"Jesus loves you. He offered His life for yours."

Lawrence gnawed on his lip. He wanted her to go away, and yet, he didn't.

"You see, He knows what you have endured, and what you are going through right now." Joanne finished her apple and wiped her hand on a napkin. She glanced over at her daughter playing on the swings. "That someone told me that Jesus knew everything about me and still loved me. He said that Jesus wanted me to be with Him in heaven, but if I died today, not accepting His free gift, His free pass into Heaven, I might not go there."

Lawrence looked across the street, but saw nothing except his very empty soul; a soul that longed to be loved.

"He asked me a very important question." Joanne waited a moment.

Lawrence took a deep breath and let it out, rattling against his nerves.

"He asked me if I knew where I would go today if I died."

Lawrence's conscience screamed, "To Hell!" He knew he was no good. Didn't his mother always tell him that?

"Do you know, Lawrence?"

Lawrence hung his head. His eyes filled with tears.

The gravel crunched in front of him.

"Mommy, why is he crying?"

"Shh Lacy, let him be."

"Mommy, is he sad because he doesn't know Jesus?"

Joanne didn't answer.

Lawrence turned to Lacy. His heart felt mangled. Was this the difference between these two and him and his mom? "Do you know Him?"

"Yes," she answered cheerfully.

"Honey, do you see the butterfly over there? Perhaps you can catch it with this." Joanne took a net from her pack and handed it to the little girl.

After Lacy scampered off Joanne put her hand on Lawrence's arm. "Lawrence, if you need someone to talk to you can come and visit my husband. He is the one who told me how I could know how to get to Heaven."

Joanne handed Lawrence a pamphlet with her husband's name and their church.

He stared at it. *Could these people help him?*

She squeezed his arm and smiled. "Would you mind if I told him about you? We'll pray for you."

Lawrence nodded.

Joanne said good bye and left to join her daughter.

He put the knife away. He no longer felt like using it.

Standing, he glanced at Joanne and Lacy. Was it possible to be happy like that?

Shoving his fists into his pockets, he walked away. Could it be possible that this Jesus could love him?

He studied his shoes as he plodded along the cobblestone walk. Maybe tomorrow he would use the knife. Or maybe tomorrow he would see Joanne's husband.

He stopped by the side of the road and looked back.

Lacy's laughter trickled across the field.

Maybe he would call Joanne's husband today. He stepped out onto the road and picked up the pace. Perhaps this man does know a better way.

Someone's Voice
A Poem of Faith

Will Someone look behind my eyes and into my heart?
I need Someone to touch my pain,
Someone whom I know will never depart,
Someone who will forgive my shame.

Can Someone tell me He cares about my deepest need?
I need Someone to reach my heart,
Someone to help me, that is all I plead.
I need Someone to touch my heart.

A new voice in the night calls out to me.
It comes from a light so faint, yet I see
I have strayed that far, is it true, could it be?
There's a bar that separates You from me.
It encircles my heart, and now I see
Lord God, in Your arms I will safely be.

A still small voice is calling out to meet my dire need.
God's gentle hand touches my heart.
Lord, break the bar that separates I plead.
I believe you're now in my heart.

Someone has looked behind my eyes and into my heart.
That Someone has healed all my pain.
I know this Someone will never depart,
Someone has forgiven my shame.

No Other God

God is powerful.

He moves mountains of pain with a single word.

He calms oceans of emotions with a wave of His hand.

He lets His perfect love settle on us with the gentleness of a dove.

No other god, modern or ancient, can do this, because no other god has

Perfect love, perfect justice, perfect mercy, or perfect holiness.

On the Creative Process

Analysis is the basis of creativity. That was my response to a man who said he could not compose artistic writing because his personality type was analytical. Any creative person must analyze his subject matter before he can create. He must also analyze his craft and, if he wishes to sell his product, he must analyze his market. The creative process contains many elements, some of which I will discuss below.

Before a person determines to be a writer, he must first have fervor to write. Fervor comes from what touches the soul and propels it into a vibrant path of emotions and intellect. Fervor coupled with inspiration brings life to words, sentences, and subjects.

Words must create a fervor within a writer - the sounds they make, the rhythms they create, the pictures they paint. They are the foundation blocks of writing. Without words a writer cannot create; without choice words a writer cannot excel.

The subject of the writer's genesis must generate a fervor to write. Energy from the love of the material drives a writer forward as he researches and analyzes the topic of his choice. If a writer does not feel passionate about the subject matter, his writing will be dull and lifeless.

The craft of writing must create fervor. A work is more than the sum of its parts; it is the perfect example of synergy. Sentence placed upon sentence, paragraph placed upon paragraph build to create instructions, illusions, and lessons that move the spirit of the reader to take action.

Upon inspiration, a writer must research. Research provides the meat for the writer's imagination to feed upon and grow into a living work.

First a writer must research his craft. He analyzes other's work and draws upon their experience. He studies the intimate details of sentence formation, paragraph generation, and scene creation. In fiction he learns plot, characterization, and setting. In non-fiction he studies the logical layout of thoughts that will teach, inspire, and motivate his reader.

Research of subject material is expedient. Facts form the foundation of any creation, whether fiction or nonfiction. From the gathering of facts ideas are generated. Sentences form to expound upon the subject until the collection of ideas and thoughts become more than the sum total of the facts.

Marketing research moderates the writer's work. Without an audience a writer's work is vain and flat. Perhaps the writer himself is the audience, but he cannot live off himself. He must determine if what he writes is wanted by someone, and he must find that someone, preferably a number of "someones".

Free-spirited writing produces the beginnings of a masterpiece. Once a writer has researched he is ready to sit and let his pen have free course over paper. Words fly from his mind to create sentences; ideas take form and drop into paragraphs; pictures of his imagination propagate images in the form of a scene or essay. The writer's love for words filters through his pen and breathes life into his work.

Editing refines the free-spirit. Editing is the cutting away of the ugly, irrelevant, and refuse created by a free-spirit gone awry. Editing is merciless yet without it the genesis of a monument to the writer's creativity would fall short of its goal.

Proofreading perfects and fine-tunes. While editing is the knife, proofreading is the writer's tool of refinement. Grammatical errors are removed with the smooth, sculpting spatula of the proofreader.

Spelling mistakes are corrected and sentence structure enhanced. Without proofreading, perfection cannot be obtained and a masterpiece will remain in its infancy.

A writer must be prepared to experience rejection and more rejection, and even more rejection. The refusal of an editor to accept a writer's submission can be an arrow shot into the heart of a young writer. The resilient will hold up against the arrows, knives, and spears of editors and readers alike. It is a part of the creative process. Without it jewels of literature would not exist.

At some point a writer will determine whether his master work should be published or tossed. He may sign a contract or he may file the piece for later revival. He may even file it in the round bin. Not every piece of clay forms into a perfect sculpture, and not every manuscript becomes a published treasure. This is a fact of writing.

Creativity draws from the imagination of a writer, and without analysis the creative process falls flat. An earthquake of editorial shaking will reveal its weak foundation and the piece will crumble to the ground. The creative process drips with the sweat of a true artist laboring over his magnum opus, and the scrutiny of his craft, subject and market bears the brunt of his free-spirited repertoire.

Where

Freedom's

Found

From Stumbling Stone to Freedom

Mrs. McDougall set the armful of firewood on the hearth and turned at the sound of the log cabin's door opening. In the doorway stood two Stony Indians dressed in buckskin and moccasins. Behind them, Andrew Sibbald emerged from a whirl of snow made alive by the wind blowing down from Northern Alberta.

The expressions on their faces sent fear coursing through her veins like wildfire, and she fought to keep the composure that had been her strength for over forty years.

Andrew Sibbald stepped around the Indians and approached her. The concerned and pained expression on his haggard face confirmed Mrs. McDougall's fears.

She knew what he was about to say. It was the very thing she had feared every time her husband went on the buffalo hunts or off on a missionary trek. She had learned to cope with this nagging apprehension all these years.

"Elizabeth," Andrew's stifled voice cut through the cold air that permeated the cabin the instant the men stepped inside. "May be you should sit down."

"No, I am fine." She locked her face, hiding the turmoil building in her heart.

Andrew cleared his throat and, with his eyes closed, spoke. "It is George."

Elizabeth's teeth clenched, and she steeled herself for the news of her husband that she, on many occasions, had unnecessarily prepared her heart to hear. This time, she knew, the Spirit's warning was real.

"A blizzard came up suddenly and he got lost. We searched everywhere, as much as it was possible, considering the weather." The words tumbled from Andrew now as though he had released a river dammed by controlled emotions. "After two weeks we found him . . . miles from where we were hunting . . . frozen. His horse was gone." He took a breath. "He's with the Lord now Elizabeth."

Andrew sank down on the crude bench in front of the fire. His shoulders rounded over his sagging chest.

Elizabeth's hand reached for the table, and she eased herself down to the bench. Death was a part of life.

Andrew looked at her with concern pulsating from his eyes. "I will go and get your sons. My wife will come, too."

"Ah Ke am," she said in Cree. "Don't worry."

Andrew smiled grimly at Elizabeth's trite response. He shook his head as if to say, "don't dismiss this as though you are not hurting." He cleared his throat. "You'll need someone around." His voice softened now from its previous strained tone. "We'll take George up to the church so you won't have to worry about moving him." Andrew pushed himself from the bench and left with the Indians in tow.

Elizabeth followed them to the door and stepped out.

The wind cruelly whipped around the corner of the cabin, snatching at the shawl that she pulled tightly around her shoulders. A glance at the northern sky told her another storm was on its way. It seemed fitting.

When the men disappeared around the bend, Elizabeth turned and stepped into the house, closing the door softly behind her. A sense of emptiness shrouded her as she paused, her hand still on the latch.

With a deep breath, she looked up and scanned the room. Her mind was bombarded with memories of George. They caused her throat to catch, and a small cry of anguish escaped. Her British upbringing refused to let her wail like the Indian women, but her heart ached no less than theirs did when they suffered loss.

Across from her were glass windows. How happy she was when George presented them to her in their first prairie home near the North Saskatchewan River. A real luxury they were. Only the Hudson's Bay chief factor's house at Fort Edmonton had glass windows.

Beneath one window stood a wood carving of George's adventure with the Iron Stone.

She smiled. George's stubborn resolve to eliminate any obstacle in the path of the Indian's becoming civilized Christians won even that battle.

"It is a stumbling stone to them," he stated the week before he removed it. "Our Lord said to pluck out our eye if it causes us to sin. Well I can't pluck out their eyes, but as sure as the snow flies I can get rid of that confounded Iron Stone!"

The Iron Stone was said to be unmovable by the Indians, and anyone who touched it would be cursed. According to Indian legend, it was placed on the hill above Battle River by the Ojibwa great spirit, Nanabozo. George likened it to Ashtoreths or Baal idols in the Bible, which kept the Israelites from serving God. Like the people in Biblical times, the Indians left offerings at the base of the Iron Stone to appeal to Nanabozo.

Elizabeth's smile dissolved. After George placed the Iron Stone in the ox cart and sent it to Ontario, the small pox plagued the McDougalls and the Indians. She lost two daughters to the ravaging disease. It took all the strength she had to nurse her own family, the people in Fort Edmonton, and the Indians. When it was over she had collapsed. Her family feared her life would be over, but God was not finished with her.

She spent many days, weeks, and even months desperately isolated while George traveled on his missionary trips. Those early days were spent in semi-terror of what the emotionally charged Indians might do. She had to wait a whole year for her house to be built because, in anger, some Indians burned the first timber for which her husband scrounged. Yet, God had been faithful.

After that winter, Elizabeth knew she must become as much the missionary as her husband. Not only by working side by side with George, but learning to be a peacemaker with the Indians while he was gone, leading informal religious services in a desperate effort to bring them to the Christ she knew and felt so close to that first winter.

"God why would you take George? The mission in Morleyville was just built. Our new home was just built!"

As though directed by an unseen hand, her gaze fell on her husband's new Bible. This leather-bound book had been presented to them in England, less than a year ago, when they completed a lecturing tour there.

A pang of pain shot through Elizabeth's tender heart.

England had been home for her at one time. The moderate climate and rolling green hills were a sharp contrast to the harsh, brown, frozen country she lived in now. England was safe. No violent men, no whiskey traders. It had laws. This wild country had none but the moral code of those who came, and many of them held the moral code of hell.

A tear escaped from her eye and trickled down her cheek, a moment of weakness in a lifetime of strength.

She caressed the Bible, and then slowly opened it. A note sat above a Psalm, and she read it.

The note was from one of the ladies who thought her dress was not suitable for touring and suggested she visit a store in her town to purchase a new one. The lady had no concept of what financial sacrifice it had taken for them to trek across Canada, then sail over the great Atlantic Ocean to bring them the good news of how God was working among the Natives of the northwest of Canada. British Society had no role in her life and to expect her to confirm to it when there was no money seemed unbearable to her.

Her cheek twitched, and a sigh escaped her lips.

Elizabeth flipped the pages and found a photograph of her husband, friends, and family standing beside the Iron Stone, now located at the Ontario Methodist College. It was carefully placed in the Bible at I Chronicles 16. Underlined was the verse, "For all the gods of the people are idols: but the Lord made the heavens."

She picked up the photograph and studied it.

Her sisters were standing behind her.

How she missed them.

They had talked until the witching hour each night of her stay in Barrie, Ontario.

She longed to return to this town where nature seemed tamer and the people were predictable. Peace prevailed in Barrie. It did not in this section of the Northwest Territories that some were now calling Alberta.

Oh, to go home, where taking a bath was not a weekly occurrence, but could happen whenever she wanted. To go home, where modern conveniences, such as well-crafted furniture with cushions, could comfort her weary body. Home, where she could feel safe from wild men and wild beasts.

Her childhood friend Lydia had clung to her before they left, begging her to stay. She insisted that something terrible was going to happen to her out in the "Wild West." Lydia, the prophet, the friend, the most intuitive of her acquaintances. She was right, something terrible had happened. George was dead.

Her hand clutched her throat, attempting to contain the emotions that threatened to take control of her senses. A deep breath harnessed them again.

Elizabeth's gaze wandered over the photograph and rested on her husband's image.

The corner of her mouth turned up as she remembered George arguing with his family about taking the photograph. This was one time that he did not get his way. His cousin was determined to go to the expense of photographing him and this stone. George wore a deep-set frown on his face, and his eyes held that familiar light of righteous anger. No, he was not at all happy with the hero-worship that prevailed at the college during his visit. He was indignant over the lack of understanding of the significance of that Iron Stone.

She sank to the bench beside the table. George would want her to carry on their work, to build the orphanage they had dreamed of, to use the gifts God had given her. George often said she had incredible insight into the needs of others and how to meet them.

Yes, God did speak to her, not verbally of course, but Spirit to spirit. He was the Spirit behind their mission and He would be the Spirit that continues the work.

Elizabeth closed the Bible, keeping the photograph clasped in her hand.

She was wrong to desire to return to Ontario. Her home was here now, among the "savages," as one lady called Elizabeth's new friends.

Her children were here. She was needed.

Elizabeth stood and began to tear the picture.

As George ridded the Indians of the Iron Stone, so she would rid herself of memories of Ontario that might entice her to run home, away from God's work. She threw the torn pieces into the fire and watched the hungry flames consume her stumbling stone.

Weariness wrapped around her, and she lowered herself on the bench by the table.

She dropped her head onto her folded arms and sobbed. Alone. No one to see. Her heart fell apart, and pain rumbled through her body and her soul.

Much later, Elizabeth wiped her eyes. Time would help her accept George's death, as she had learned to accept so many other terrible things that marked her life in this harsh, she sighed, yet beautiful land. May God grant her the strength to do so!

Two days later, Elizabeth stood beside her husband's grave where he was buried in his buckskins and moccasins, and took comfort in the knowledge that he ministered in death as he did in life. Around her stood many Stony Indians, honoring this brave man who had stolen the Iron Stone and brought them a freedom they had never known before. She would continue that work of freedom.

Elisha, the Widow, and the Jars

God did not forget those who were faithful to Him when Israel turned to other gods. God's kindness and abundant mercy provided for the widow and her boys. Scripture doesn't tell us how old the boys were or what they were really like, but I imagine they were somewhat like Jehoram and Eli. I retell this story from the eyes of the youngest son. It is a fictional account. I hope you will read the real story from God's Word (II Kings 4:1-7).

Jehoram huddled beside his brother Eli in the darkest corner of the house. His mother's voice floated on the dry air as she spoke to the rich man from Jerusalem. "We'll find a way."

"Tomorrow." Adonai Boaz's voice thundered.

Jehoram shuddered. He heard the man's footsteps retreat and nudged Eli.

His brother grunted and uncurled his long legs. "Come on." Eli pulled Jehoram's hand. "We've got to help Mother."

Jehoram's short, five year old legs ached after sitting in the cramped corner so long. His stomach ached too. He looked at his skinny brother's bony body and wondered if his bones stuck out the same way.

"Eli," his mother said, her voice crisp and prickled with worry.

The boys stepped out of the house. The cold wind whipped Jehoram's tattered clothes and he shivered.

"I am going to see the holy man, Master Elisha. Stay here and hide our last pot of oil. Do not leave. Hide in the house. Do you understand?"

"Yes, Mother." Eli straightened. He was tall for his ten years of age.

Jehoram licked his lips. Eli looked like their father. Jehoram sniffled and wiped his nose. Father wouldn't have let that Adonai Boaz man come around.

"Jehoram, you are coming with me." his mother smoothed his ruffled hair with her bony fingers. Her lips smiled, but her eyes looked sad. "We'll be back before sunset."

Jehoram wiggled his toes in the dirt. "Mother?"

"Yes?"

"What did Adonai Boaz want?"

Mother stood still for a moment. Her mouth twitched. "Don't worry about him, son." She held out her hand.

Jehoram scratched his arm, and then put his hand into hers.

After walking down the dusty street, past camels with heavy loads and many people calling to them to buy their wares, Jehoram and his mother stopped at a tent. A tall, bald man with a colorful robe that had purple tassels on the bottom came out of the tent.

Jehoram curled his toes and wondered how a man could have such big feet.

Jehoram's mother fell to her knees, pulling him with her.

Sharp rocks poked into his hands. He minded his mother though, and did not cry out.

The scent of roasted barley came from the fire nearby and Jehoram's mouth watered. His stomach growled. He ate the last bit of bread last night, and he had asked when Mother would get something more. Mother had shushed him and Eli kicked him in the shin. He decided he better not ask again.

"Your servant, my husband, is dead." Mother's voice cracked.

Jehoram's own eyes filled with tears.

"And you know that your servant did fear the Lord."

A tear splattered on the ground sending small billows of dust across Jehoram's hand. He wiped his eyes.

"And the creditor—" Mother choked. Her hand that held Jehoram's trembled.

"He is come to take unto him my two sons to be bondmen."

Jehoram gripped Mother's hand hard. So that was why Adonai Boaz came to their house. He had a big ugly nose and sounded mean. He would not be nice to serve.

"What shall I do for you?" Master Elisha's voice came soft and gentle.

117

Jehoram felt Mother shake like the scared rabbit he caught last week.

"Tell me—" Master Elisha said, his voice not louder than a whisper "—what have you in your house?"

Jehoram wrinkled his nose. Did the holy man want something from them too? Jehoram frowned. They had nothing to give. Maybe this man wasn't so nice.

Mother whispered in a voice that sounded like a hollow, empty well. "Your handmaid has not anything in the house save a pot of oil."

Was Mother going to give the holy man their last pot of oil?

"Go, borrow vessels abroad of all your neighbors, even empty ones. Borrow not a few. And when you come into your house, shut the door behind you and your sons, and pour out into all those vessels, and you shall set aside what is full."

Jehoram lifted his head and looked at the holy man of God. He wiggled his nose. What did Master Elisha think they would do with all those pots? They can't eat them and they had nothing to put into them.

Master Elisha's soft brown eyes twinkled and he smiled at Jehoram, but Jehoram did not smile back.

What a silly old man.

Mother stood up and pulled on Jehoram's hand. "Come, we have work to do."

He got up and followed his mother.

"Jehoram, I want you to go to all our neighbors south of town and ask them for jars. Hurry now, we've not much time before sunset."

He pulled on his ear and wiped his hands on his robes, while watching his toes wiggle in the dirt.

"Go on now, son."

He walked down the street to Noami's house while his mother hurried toward their house. After kicking a stone, he looked back at Master Elisha. What did the holy man of God think would happen? He shrugged his shoulders and turned to head to the small house at the end of the street.

When Jehoram reached Noami's gate he called out.

"Why Jehoram, what are you doing?" asked Noami in her nasal voice that sounded to him like she stuck plugs into her nostrils.

"Mother told me to ask you for all the jars and vessels you have."

Noami raised her eyebrows, "Why?"

He shrugged and rubbed his nose.

118

She sighed. "Well, come in and get those empty ones by the wall. Use that wheelbarrow over by the table to carry them home."

"Thank you," He said and smiled. It would be fun to push the wheelbarrow.

He filled the wheelbarrow with jars and then went to Sarah's, Rachel's and Moriah's. He filled the wheelbarrow up four times before sunset. When he brought the last wheelbarrow load home, he laughed at their overflowing house.

"Mother, we don't have any place to stand." He clapped his hands.

"Eli, shut the door," said Mother with her hands on her hips, surveying the clutter of empty jars.

Eli closed the door.

Light filtered through the lattice on the window, and danced on the brown vessels of various shapes and sizes.

Jehoram shuffled his feet on the dirt floor, wondering what would happen next. He heard about Master Elisha healing the water at Jericho. Samuel, the boy next door, said that Master Elisha was even mightier than Master Elijah. Will something amazing happen now? Jehoram bounced on the balls of his feet, watching his mother pick up their one small jar of oil and begin to pour it into Noami's large plain brown jar.

Jehoram's eyes grew wide as the jar filled to the top and his mother began to fill the next vessel. It filled to the brim too.

Jehoram clapped and hopped, and giggled and chortled as every jar in the house filled to the brim with oil.

"Eli, bring me another vessel."

"Mother, there is not another vessel." Eli's voice bounced like a sheepskin ball.

Mother laughed and cried and picked Jehoram up. She held Jehoram in a tight embrace and Eli held them both. Eli's cheeks sparkled like rain drops on a leaf.

"It is a miracle boys!" Mother's voice rang with joy. She set Jehoram down. "Listen. I want you both to stay in the house with the door closed."

"Where are you going Mother?" Jehoram asked as he followed her to the door, carefully weaving through the clutter of jars.

"I''m going to see Master Elisha."

"May I come, please?"

"Stay here son, I'll be back soon." She stepped out the door and closed it.

Jehoram heard the padding of her footsteps, hurrying down the dirt street.

"Come on Jehoram." Eli pulled on his arm and opened the door. "Let's follow."

"But Mother said . . ."

"Close the door and be quiet. Don't you want to know what Master Elisha says?"

Of course Jehoram did. He closed the door.

The sun had set and dark shadows crept into their courtyard. He hurried after Eli who slinked along the shadow of the courtyard wall.

The street no longer seemed friendly. Houses and shops stood dark.

Jehoram grasped the back of Eli's tunic. He didn't want to get lost.

They pulled up behind the holy man's tent, and Jehoram saw his mother face down before Master Elisha. Her voice tinkled with joy and excitement. "The vessels are filled with oil!"

Master Elisha's soft voice filtered through the sounds of bleating sheep. "Go, sell the oil, and pay your debt, and live you and your children on the rest."

Jehoram felt giddy.

Eli pulled on him and urged him to hurry back to their house through the shadows. When they got home they fell against the wall and roared in laughter, punching each other with delight. They could hardly wait until tomorrow, when they could get ugly, old Adonai Boaz off their mother's back. Wouldn't he be surprised!

A Faith that Saves

But they cried, saying, Crucify Him, crucify Him. And he said unto them the third time, Why, what evil hath He done? I have found no cause of death in Him: I will therefore chastise Him, and let Him go . . .
.

And when they were come to the place, which is called Calvary, there they crucified Him, and the malefactors, one on the right hand, and the other on the left. Then said Jesus, Father, forgive them; for they know not what they do. And they parted his raiment, and cast lots.
. . . And he said unto Jesus, Lord, remember me when Thou comest into Thy kingdom. And Jesus said unto him, Verily I say unto thee, To day shalt thou be with Me in paradise.

Luke 23:21-43

"Crucify him!" The crowd cried.
Samuel burned with anger.
"Crucify him!"
Samuel locked his jaw. Why didn't Jesus do something?
Someone shoved Samuel from behind and knocked him down on the stony road.
Sharp pain shot through his raw knees.
"Get up thief!" A soldier yanked on his hair.
Samuel gasped and shut his eyes tight against the pain.

"You should be honored." the soldier's rough mocking voice resonated through Samuel's pain-filled head. "You hang with the King of the Jews today."

A rough post slammed against his shoulders.

Samuel gagged as the wind left his lungs. He stumbled but did not fall.

Two soldiers pulled him up by his arms and tied him to the post.

His heart pounded so hard it would surely leave his chest. He hissed through clenched teeth at the men holding him.

The smell of urine and vomit that whiffed into his nostrils sent his stomach into a series of lurches.

He looked up to see his partner enduring the same treatment as he, but from Eli's mouth poured out a flood of vile words.

A soldier pushed Samuel forward.

He coughed and staggered.

Eli's mouth never stopped with its vile eruptions, just as it never did before they were caught.

He hated his partner. If it were not for Eli and his boastings about their exploits, they would never have been caught.

Weeping swirled around him like a rainstorm as the soldiers pushed Samuel into the crowd.

He prayed his mother would not be there. A pang shot through his heart. His dear sweet mother should not have had such a worthless son.

"Daughters of Jerusalem." The rasping voice of Jesus penetrated his misery, and he twisted his neck to see the man some called the Messiah, but pain blackened his vision. "Weep not for Me, but for yourselves."

A blow on his back sent Samuel staggering forward.

He gasped as the muscles in his arms tore. Pinned to the patibulum of the cross, his arms could not move to keep his balance.

If Jesus was who He said He was, why would He not save Himself?

A rough hand whipped Samuel around and before him loomed the large Roman nose of a centurion. A blow to the back of his knees sent him backward, gasping.

Pain streaked up and down his spine as he thudded against a post. He cried out, protesting the agony that accosted him.

Wham, clink. A hammer hitting a spike. The sound echoed in his head, vibrating off every nerve.

His skin turned cold as panic surged through his body. He fought against the bonds that held him in place.

Minutes later he lay gasping, sweating, and shivering.

Cries of mockery rang out around him.

His gaze followed the long ropes that yanked and jerked up the cross upon which he laid. The actions drifting in a fog as his consciousness wavered.

He smelled the bitter scent of gall. Strange, how his senses seemed keener than normal.

"He saved others: Himself He cannot save. If He be the King of Israel, let Him now come down from the cross, and we will believe Him!" The gruff, angry voice sliced through the crisp morning air. A volley of angry voices followed it.

Samuel pushed himself up against the foot rest and gasped for breath. "Some King of the Jews!" he gasped, angered that he too would die.

"Father, forgive them for they know not what they do." The wobbly voice of the dying Man rose above the crowd's railing.

"If You be the King of the Jews save thyself." the brutal bass voice of a soldier thundered out.

A memory of a palsy man lowered into Eli's parents' house flashed before Samuel. Jesus had forgiven that man too. Samuel pulled himself up by the arms.

Hot searing pain shot through his body as he gasped for breath.

He remembered a weasel-like little scribe saying, "Who can forgive sins, but God only?"

Samuel's body shivered and sweat trickled down his nose. He shook his head.

"If You be Christ, save Yourself and us!" Eli's voice croaked, and Samuel's anger spiked. This fool of a man led him into a life of crime, how could he speak like that to Jesus?

"Do not you fear God, seeing you are in the same condemnation?" Samuel bellowed and coughed up blood. He choked and wheezed and pulled himself up for another breath. "And we indeed justly; for we receive the due reward of our deeds."

Samuel's heart pounded harder as his mind raced over the life of Jesus that he knew . . . talks in the temple and in the streets of

His coming kingdom; compassion He showed to people Samuel knew. "But this man has done nothing amiss."

Shame washed over him as the knowledge of his own worthless, wicked life glared at him through his memories. He knew then, who Jesus was. He knew Jesus could only be the Messiah spoken of in Scripture. "Lord, remember me when You come into Your kingdom."

Jesus turned to him, blood streamed down his face. He pushed up and gasped for breath and said, "Verily I say unto you, today shall you be with Me in paradise."

Samuel coughed and wheezed and choked, but peace covered over his pain. He was forgiven.

#

This is a fictional account of how the thief on the cross might have seen things, but his faith and his salvation are not fictional. Salvation is a simple thing often made complex by the minds of men who try to reason it out.

Yet one man, in the last moments of his life received it, despite his wickedness. The thief on the cross recognized his position, confessed his sins, and asked Jesus to remember him. He recognized that Jesus was perfect. How much did he know about Jesus? Enough to know that He was without sin. He believed in God, and he knew enough to call Jesus Lord. Likely he did not fully understand the four spiritual laws quoted today, but he knew enough to believe and to ask Jesus to remember him. On that faith, Jesus chose him to come with Him into paradise.

In summary, the thief:
1. Acknowledged he was a sinner (Luke 23:40-41)
2. Understood that he deserved the punishment for his sins (Luke 23:41)
3. Acknowledge who Jesus was (Luke 23:42)
4. Asked Jesus to remember him (admitting that he would not be going to the same place Jesus would be and showing a longing to have Jesus' mercy) (Luke 23:42)
5. Received Jesus assurance that he was saved (Luke 23:43)

We too can experience salvation from our sins and from the fire of hell as this thief did, if we follow his example.

Do you know where you will go when you die? Email me at lynnsquire@gmail.com if you have any questions.

The Woman with the Lamborghini

Shenaii stumbled down the stairs of the Good Shepherd Catholic Church in Hollywood. The chanting of monastic music from morning mass rang in her ears. She wanted to scream. Incense still clung to her, feeding on her guilt like mold on cheese. Even confession gave her no relief.

Climbing into her Lamborghini, she gritted her teeth and decided it better to leave God behind than to keep up this facade of faith. She inserted the key into the ignition and turned it. Click. She turned it again. Click.

Her chest bulged inside her, and she held her breath, ready to explode. Pounding on the steering wheel with the fury of a wild man she screamed. "Are you cursing the car too, God?"

A sharp cramp crumpled her. Her own womb condemned her. Tears pooled in her eyes, threatening to spill over onto her cheeks. She wrapped her arm around her abdomen. "They said it wouldn't hurt." She squealed through a clenched jaw.

Someone knocked on the window.

Startled, she quickly wiped her eyes and stared at the gray floor of her car while the pain subsided. This was supposed to be a quiet street.

Another knock and a bass voice said, "Are you alright?"

She lifted her head and saw a dark-haired, young man with a concerned look etched on his face.

Why wouldn't he go away and leave her alone?

He grasped the door handle.

She should push the lock down, but . . . her problem wasn't his fault. He was trying to be nice, after all. She took a deep breath, opened the door, and stepped out.

The young man's brown eyes opened wide in recognition. Before he spoke, he cleared his throat. "Would you mind having coffee with me?"

Her lip curled in disgust. Not another fan looking for something to tell his friends back home. She glowered at him. His clothes were cheap, Wal-Mart purchases. The kind her mother forced her to wear when she was a girl.

Her glare stopped at his face. Sincere concern etched on his brow accentuated the depth of charity in his eyes.

Unnerved by his expression, she cast her eyes downward and saw the Bible in his hand.

She puffed out a quick breath. Looking away from the Bible, she locked her attention on his eyes. "No doubt you know who I am. What does the likes of you want with me? I thought Bible Thumpers were repulsed by movie stars such as myself."

The man met her angry stare with a steady gaze. "If you knew what we 'Bible Thumpers' had to offer, you would be coming to us and asking for the gift we would share with you," His tone remained calm and composed.

She lifted her chin. It would be his due if she gave in to the displeasure that she displayed, but in all honesty, his words intrigued her. "What could you offer me—" she waved her hand over her LP640 Roadster, "—that I don't already have?"

He tilted his head to glance at the silver Lamborghini and returned his focus to her. His unwavering expression unsettled her. No man looked at her car without wanting to look under its hood.

She narrowed her eyes. "You don't even have money enough to buy decent clothes, so of course you wouldn't be interested in the car."

"I have riches beyond yours. Your riches will never satisfy you, but my riches are of immeasurable value, and satisfy my deepest longing. Those that have riches like mine have no need to seek comfort in fancy cars, clothes, and mansions."

She snorted, but her heart called her a hypocrite. She turned and stroked the top of her vehicle. All her riches had only brought her more men. More men meant more trouble. Not even the priest at the

Good Shepherd could bring her comfort. Instead he troubled her soul. She whispered, "I would trade my riches for a peace that satisfied."

"Go call your husband."

She huffed. "I'm divorced."

"That's right." The young man nodded. "You've been divorced five times, if I recall correctly, and you are not married to the man you live with now."

"Do you condemn me?"

The man tipped his head to the side. "It is not my place to."

"I just came out of the Good Shepherd Church. They condemned me. I thought all Christians did."

He looked down at his feet and groaned.

Surely he would leave now.

But after a moment he looked up at her. Narrowing his eyes, he said, "You are worshipping what you don't know. Jesus Christ's gift of salvation is free, for everyone, whether murderers or liars."

She leaned back sharply and ran her finger along the edge of her car's window. *What do I worship? I thought . . . I thought I could reach God at this place.*

What did he know about her? She stiffened and tapped the roof of her car with her index finger. *I am a murderer and a liar.* Her conscience berated her. She struggled to breathe. "I thought you had to be good to be saved."

The young man studied her face.

She squirmed. What did he see? Could he know what she did yesterday?

"The Bible tells us that Abraham believed, and God counted it as righteousness. It says all our righteousness is as filthy rags, but if we call upon the name of the Lord, we will be saved."

She licked her lips. Her mind wanted to block his words, but something else, in her innermost self, prodded her to meet his eyes.

He continued, "Romans 10:9-10 says 'That if thou shalt confess with thy mouth the Lord Jesus, and shall believe in thine heart that God hath raised Him from the dead, thou shalt be saved. For with the heart man believeth unto righteousness, and with the mouth confession is made unto salvation."

A battle of wills exploded inside her. One side denied the young man's words; the other longed for it to be true. Her nerves stretched tight. She gave a ragged breath, and then whispered, "All I do is believe, and I will find this peace you have?"

128

"Do you want to be saved from your sins?"

"Yes!" the answer came on an exhalation. Could she be released from the grip her lifestyle had over her? Could she be freed from the chains of guilt?

The voice of hope rose above the voice of doubt. She listened. Short, quick breaths led to the release of years of anxiety. Her heart pumped as though new blood coursed through her veins. "Yes!" She repeated, louder this time. "Could it be possible . . . even for me?"

"Simply accept His gift . . . His payment for your sins. Jesus died on the cross, bearing the punishment you deserved for your sins. Believe that He died for you, was buried, and conquered death. He is alive today. Believe and He will make you free."

Her chest swelled to openness. She put her hands on the young man's shoulders. "Pray for me, that Jesus would find me acceptable."

The man shook his head. "He already loves you. All He asks is that you take what He is offering." He gently removed her hands from his shoulders. "Would you like to confess to Him your faith?"

Her stomach twisted and her face emptied of blood. Could Jesus really mean it? *I am a murderer, an adulterer, a . . . and He loved me enough to take away all that, at the price of death?*

She lowered herself to her knees and clasped her hands over her face. "Dear Jesus." A sob escaped and tears rolled down her cheeks. "I am a horrible sinner."

The sound of her beating heart thundered in her head. She knew Jesus was real. She could feel Him, like as if He were stirring her very spirit. Could it be possible that by just believing He would bring peace to her life?

Her clammy hands pressed against her eyes. *I must choose to have faith.* "I believe what this man said. Dear Jesus."

A wonderful warmth pushed a smile on her face, and a calm flowed over her. "I believe you paid for my sins. I believe you are alive today."

She whimpered. "Please forgive me."

In her heart billowed a conviction to change, to cast aside her life as she had lived it. She pressed her hands against her eyes as she gasped, grasping the meaning of this. "Please help me to live for you."

A car drove past.

She tingled with the beginnings of joy and pushed herself up from the ground. *I'm saved.* The words thundered in her soul. Newness of life flowed over her with a peace she never before experienced. She looked at the young man.

He grinned from ear to ear, and extended his hand.

She clasped it.

"Welcome to the family," he said.

Sandy's Prayer

Sandy fell before the altar. Her heart burned. Why had her world fallen apart? Her only son died—hit by a sports car on his way to school. The funeral costs and the muddled arrangements drove another wedge between her and the man she loved, causing him to leave as well. She pressed her forehead against the rough, blue carpet at the foot of the altar.

Never had she felt more abandoned. God did not care. How could He care? Look at her.

She wiped at tear off her cheek.

The mistakes she made—they were insurmountable. If only she had not rushed into her business. If only she had not longed for the comforts she saw in others' homes.

Her shoulders crumpled. The weight of her own useless efforts to better herself pressed heavy upon her.

"I had thought I owned the world," she whispered.

Strong winds battered the stain glass windows, battering her soul as well. A damp smell from the vicious storm lingered in the sanctuary.

Sandy whimpered.

The clattering, ripping, sounds of the gale echoed through the great hall.

She shuddered; her own life ripped by the prevailing winds of bad judgment. She felt lost, adrift in the squall of her own miserable decisions. *Oh Lord, what have I done?*

An onslaught of pounding, torrential rain answered her cry.

Her tears joined the downpour.

Do you know who I am, child? No voice spoke.

Sandy sunk lower. There was no audible voice, but she heard it. It rolled over her soul like the clouds that rolled across the dark sky. "Oh God, what have I done?"

Child, do you know who I am?

Sandy dug her fingernails into the carpet fibers. "Yes, Lord."

You call me Lord, but do you know who I am?

Sandy gritted her teeth and squeezed her eyes tight against the pain of admission. "Lord?"

Child, have you lived with the knowledge of who I am in your heart?

"What do you mean, Lord?" The moment she asked guilt swept over her like a wave. Memories of arguments and hateful thoughts passed before her, playing out her life on the screen of her subconscious. Strife she had stirred between her and her husband, envious feelings of others wealth, discord she had evoked through her own desire to be valued: these did not reflect a knowledge of God. She stretched out, prostrate before her God. "Lord, I have sinned."

How often do we pray out of the burden of our hearts? Do we only pray when the storms batter our lives? God calls us into a close and intimate relationship with Him. He cares about the details of our lives, but He also cares that we know Him and all that He is.

Prayer is a form of worship. Reflecting on God's attributes is a vital part of the process. Conversing in intimate conversation with the great I Am defines this important act. While we are told to let our requests be made known to God (Philippians 4:6), we must not leave the former undone.

Our prayer life discloses our relationship with God. Prayer must become more than bowing our heads, folding our hands, and closing our eyes. It must become an emptying of our mind of all else but the things we desire to present to God and the thoughts toward Him that bring Him honor and glory.

God hears our every thought. We need to comprehend that these thoughts can be like a prayer, communicating to Him in a manner that either draws us to Him or drives us away (Psalms 94:11).

Philippians 4:4-8 reveals there is a relationship between our prayers and our thought life.

> v. 4 - Rejoicing in the Lord prepares your mind and your heart to enter into His presence.

v.5 - The Lord is at hand; what have you done in your life to demonstrate your knowledge of this? Have you lived a life not driven by passions and indulgences, but in a calmness of mind? Enter into prayer from a life of moderation seen by all men. What you do before you pray affects your time of communion with the Holy and Righteous Judge, the Great I Am.

v.6 - Make your requests to Him with thanksgiving. Being thankful demonstrates humility and an acknowledgement that all good things come from Him.

v.7 - God's peace guards our hearts and minds. Stay before Him, until you can leave your prayer closet with this awesome truth ruling your heart and mind.

v.8 - Depart from your prayer time with your mind centered on what is true, honest, just, pure, lovely, virtuous, and praiseworthy.

Prayer time is a battleground. II Corinthians 10:5 says: "Casting down imaginations, and every high thing that exalteth itself against the knowledge of God, and bringing into captivity every thought to the obedience of Christ." Without prayer being directed to the praise, glory, and honor of the Almighty, we will lose the battle and leave the field defeated.

Rescued from Death

Exiled from life,
Freed from sin,
Given Eternity.

Exiled from life,
Lost in the dark,
Hopelessly caught.

Freed from sin,
Loosed from lies,
Liberated from evil.

Given Eternity,
Grace abounds,
True Life renewed forever.

The Truth of the Matter

"But ye should say, Why persecute we him, seeing the root of the matter is found in me?" Job 19:28 (King James Version)

Job endured great loss and physical pain yet spoke of his faith even though his friends persecuted him. His friends hurt him with words. In their desire to answer why Job went through these trials, they tore him down and built themselves up. They knew it all. They reasoned Job must have committed horrendous sins to receive the wrath of God; his family and riches ripped from him, and his body infected with stinking, oozing sores.

Job wanted his friends' pity, not persecution. He wanted them to see him as faithful, not wicked. He spoke forcefully against their accusations. His friends could not understand. They did not live his life. They did not see the things he saw, nor felt the things he felt. They did not experience life as he did, and they certainly did not know his innermost thoughts and feelings. Only God and Job would know the wrongs Job may have committed, and his friends were foolish to think they were righteous enough or wise enough to discover them.

Rarely is the truth of a matter found on the surface. Often truth lives buried deep beneath perceptions, deceptions, and emotions. How often have we jumped to conclusions, judging another's sufferings by our limited perception and our limited knowledge? Wisdom guides us to be humble, perhaps even for this simple fact: some day we may be lying on our beds of tragedy, and what would we want said to us?

Suggested Bible Reading: Job 1-42

On the Road to Destruction

For thy violence against thy brother Jacob shame shall cover thee, and thou shalt be cut off for ever. Obadiah 1:10

Obadiah is a prophet of God to the Edomites. The Edomites were descendants of Esau, the brother to Jacob who was father of the Israelites. Obadiah's message – they will be destroyed.

Why? Edom sided with Israel's enemies and rejoiced when the Israelites were taken captive. Edom, in its pride, could not see that their own destruction was eminent. God judged them, and they fell at the hands of the very people they allied themselves with against Israel.

How often do we tell ourselves we are better than another? We point our fingers saying, "I'd never do that." Or, "They caused their own trouble."

Anyone who has been hurt by the scorn of others can depend on God settling the score. The Bible tells us "for God resisteth the proud, and giveth grace to the humble." (I Peter 5:5b). We need to take care that we are not the ones in need of being humbled.

Is Your Water Boiling?

When thou passest through the waters, I will be with thee; and through the rivers, they shall not overflow thee: when thou walkest through the fire, thou shalt not be burned; neither shall the flame kindle upon thee. Isaiah 43:2

The other night, after saying our bedtime prayers, my daughter asked me why we have to go through trials—a difficult question indeed. How often do we slip into the mentality that life should be a bowl of cherries without the pits? Yet God didn't promise us that.

He did, however, promise His redeemed that He would be there with us as we go through those troublesome times. But that doesn't answer why. That merely tells us where He is.

Job asked a similar question and God responded with a series of questions proving that He indeed was sovereign. The Israelites time and again turned from God, suffered trials, repented, and were rescued. Why? That they might know the Lord their God (Ezekiel 23:49).

The reason for suffering is difficult for the person experiencing it to discern. Sometimes they are convicted of a sin; sometimes they know it is the result of another's actions or words against them; and sometimes it is simply an act of fate. Yet often the conclusions are not readily drawn from the circumstances. Whatever the suffering, one truth prevails, and that is God's love and desire for each person to draw closer to Him.

When I spoke with my daughter, my own heart was pricked as I recalled times in my life when I thought all was lost. It was in those dark hours that I pleaded with God to save me and to end my misery. But with the perspective of time, I can look back and see how each pain in life, each harm placed in my way, each strife, and each trial revealed a part of God that I did not understand or was unaware of before. Each situation exposed God's abiding love, even when the situation incited emotional or physical pain.

For my daughter, I likened trials to a pot of water. Boiled water has an abundance of uses. It enables you to make tea or pasta, or even to sterilize a baby's bottle. Before the water can be useful in these ways, however, it must get hot.

Sometimes God wants to do something with us either in the present or in the future, and in order to prepare us for that service He first must set us on the fire. When the boiling point happens steam is released, germs are killed, and impurities are separated from the water. When we experience trials that burn us or make us hot, we can be assured through God's Word that He is going to bring us through it with a greater purpose in mind, even if it was only that we know more of Him and all His provision.

That the trial of your faith, being much more precious than of gold that perisheth, though it be tried with fire, might be found unto praise and honour and glory at the appearing of Jesus Christ: I Peter 1:7

Why must we endure trials and hardships? That we might know God and all that He is, and that we might be purified and prepared for a future purpose.

How comforting this statement is depends on where our focus lies. If our focus is on our own comfort and personal desires, then no, this is not comforting. However, if our focus is on the Lord, humbling ourselves by recognizing who we are and who He is, then what a tremendous comfort it is to know that the all-powerful, all-knowing, sovereign God is working to make the most out of us.

Is your pot boiling? Then praise the Lord, He's at work in your life. Let Him take you along for His praise and honor and glory—you never know you might become a perfect cup of tea.

The Hope

Often I hear people speak of the hardships of war, the mistakes of our leadership, and the horrors of this world. Sometimes we can overwhelm ourselves with these negative images.

There is so much evil in the world that it can easily become the focus of our thoughts and fears. Yet, I know the faithfulness of God. I have experienced His miracles of turning bad into good, and, though I know the world is going to get worse before it gets better, I can rest upon His abundant grace and mercies (which are new every morning).

I believe that life in this world must get worse before life gets better, and when it does get better, wow! It will be beyond anything we can imagine.

"And I saw a new heaven and a new earth: for the first heaven and the first earth were passed away; and there was no more sea. ... And I heard a great voice out of heaven saying, Behold, the tabernacle of God is with men, and he will dwell with them, and they shall be his people, and God himself shall be with them, and be their God. And God shall wipe away all tears from their eyes; and there shall be no more death, neither sorrow, nor crying, neither shall there be any more pain: for the former things are passed away. And He that sat upon the throne said, Behold, I make all things new." Revelations 21:1, 3-5a

I Laid Me Down and Slept

I laid me down and slept; I awaked; for the Lord sustained me. Psalm 3:5 (*KJV*)

A scream cuts through the dark and silence of the night. A mother runs to her child's side. Her child sits up straight and stiff. A night terror had engulfed the child's dream world.

A man shoots up straight from his bed. His labored breathing matches his sweat-soaked pajamas. A memory of the past darkened his dreams and drew him into a recollection of the terrors of war.

King David had reasons for sleepless nights. He had faced giants, dodged spears, and now he ran for his life, away from his own son. Yet, he lay down and slept. He knew who his shield was; he knew who his avenger was; he knew God was on his side. Experience proved God could and would sustain him and he trusted God would hear his prayers.

Peace of mind is not found in human solutions. How often have I said, "if only this or if only that, then I would have peace"? How often have I longed for miracles that I would never see? How often have I sought for peace through my own limited vision of what the possibilities might be?

Peace comes not by human explication. I cannot explain away a problem God designed. I cannot search for an answer that a human cannot understand.

Peace comes when I rest upon the knowledge of a Loving Savior and an Almighty Creator. Disasters come and may even stay, but there is a place that protects my soul. David did not say, I slept and then God saved me. He said "I slept; I awaked; for the Lord *sustained* me." God propped him up and gave him something solid to lean upon. David let his soul rest in this. He chose not to be afraid because he knew the One who seals up the hand of man (Job 37:7); the One who rules over all.

In times of crisis and stress we can be as David and lean on the Creator who hears our prayer. We may not find salvation from our sorrows in this world, but if we believe in Jesus Christ as our personal Savior, we can know for sure that we will find relief on the other shore—and we can rest in this.

Encountering Stress
Encountering God

Though out for a celebration supper, I felt like crying. We finally received an offer for our condominium. Unfortunately, the offer for our condo came several thousand dollars lower than our asking price, which was forty thousand dollars less than what we paid. Our savings, dedicated to preparing for our coming baby, would be used to cover closing costs.

My husband, content that God's hands held us, tried to reassure me that we were doing the right thing. "No one would buy a leaky condo," he told me. "It is a miracle we are able to sell at all."

Closing my eyes, I tried to squeeze the tension away. Through clenched teeth I said, "Can we afford to pay the realtor and legal fees? And will we be able to find a place this weekend to rent?"

The potential new owners wanted to take possession at the first of the month, only two weeks away. My weak faith failed to see God's provision.

The next day I searched the papers and scoured the church bulletin board for places to rent. There seemed little hope of finding anything since university and college students would be looking as well. For $800 plus utilities a hole in the ground was considered a steal, though nearly double our mortgage payment. The situation seemed hopeless.

Sunday afternoon, after a fruitless Saturday of walking through dark basement suites, dingy houses, and smelly apartments, I found myself further discouraged by a dwindling number of places left to rent. I fell before God, begging for an affordable place with good landlords where I would feel comfortable introducing our unborn baby to the world.

Praise the Lord, God answered my prayer with my next telephone call. A retired Christian couple sought to rent out their lovely, bright, clean basement suite to a couple just like us! We gave them a check for a damage deposit and rejoiced.

Two days later our realtor called and punctured a hole in my joy. The buyers were second-guessing their decision. We might lose the sale. Anxiety set in and my emotions, already volatile from pregnancy, took me on a wild rollercoaster ride. What was God doing?

Five very long, prayer-filled days later we signed the papers, and the sale closed. In a week we packed and moved to our new home, rejoicing.

My first morning devotions in our new place confirmed God's control and His desire to teach me to trust Him. "But my God shall supply all your need according to His riches in glory by Christ Jesus" (Philippians 4:19 KJV).

As the meaning of the verse took root, I laughed aloud, and then laughed even more as I looked over two weeks of God's provision. My prayer time filled with thanksgiving and the knowledge that future financial worries could be cast onto God's broad shoulders. We may have lost over forty thousand dollars due to poor construction of our first home, but we have a very wealthy Heavenly Father who provides for our every need.

The Religion of Mother Earth
Save the World Campaign

HGTV has their "Save the World Campaign." They preach their gospel of environmental awareness, telling us that if we do our part we will change the world. Unfortunately they believe a lie, and they are leading others to believe the same.

Jesus had His own "Save the World Campaign." He came preaching the coming of the Kingdom of God. He told us to repent. He told us to believe in Him, and then He gave His life for us. Being the Creator, He was not concerned about Global Warming, or whales dying, or carbon emissions. His concern was with the souls of mankind. His concern was with our relationship with Him (not earth). He took this campaign so serious that He gave his life for it.

I will likely continue to recycle. The price of gas has caused me to drive less. The cost of watering my lawn keeps me from overwatering. But if sending out thousands of flyers on paper will bring one person to know the salvation found only in the Lord Jesus Christ, then every penny I spent on those flyers is worth it. If driving across the nation will lead one child to a saving knowledge of Jesus Christ, then every carbon emission and every drop of fossil fuel is worth it.

HGTV can have their "Save the World Campaign" and get a temporal result. I chose to go with God's campaign, and I am confident it will have an eternal result of infinitely greater value.

In Search of the Wii

Jesus saith unto him, I am the way, the truth, and the life: no man cometh unto the Father, but by me. John 14:6

My parents wanted to buy my children a Wii for Christmas, and so began our hunt for a console. We searched every store that sold electronics. We surfed the web for every possible location. In vain we called stores on a daily basis, hoping to catch a console as it was delivered. Instead, all we find were Wii games and accessories—all useless without the console.

These stores remind me of so many religious assemblies. Many religious groups purport to have the accessories to life (the way to peace, a comfortable and fun community, programs to entertain and teach good values). They advertise that their form of worship or religion will give you all you need to live a fulfilled and complete life, or to help you fulfill your spiritual needs.

Yet they fail to present the Truth. They sell the accessories, but fail to tell you of your need to connect with Jesus through faith. They sell the games, but fail to mention that His death, burial and resurrection provide the only payment for our sin and for our freedom from sin's mastery over us. There is only one way to peace with God; there is only one way to play the true game of life; and that is through the Lord Jesus Christ.

What does your assembly of worshippers offer? Merely accessories and games that profess to give you deep satisfaction? Or does it present the true Gospel in which true peace and eternal life can be found? If it doesn't offer this, then the games and accessories they do offer are nothing more than wall art for a failing store. You need the console; you need Jesus.

Heaven is a Wonderful Place

"And he showed me a pure river of water of life, clear as crystal, proceeding out of the throne of God and of the Lamb. In the midst of the street of it, and on either side of the river, was there the tree of life, which bare twelve manner of fruits, and yielded her fruit every month: and the leaves of the tree were for the healing of the nations. And there shall be no more curse: but the throne of God and the Lamb shall be in it; and His servants shall serve Him: and they shall see His Face; and His name shall be in their foreheads. And there shall be no night there; and they need no candle, neither light of the sun; for the Lord God giveth them light: and they shall reign for ever and ever." Revelations 22:1-5

If we were to solve the problem of pollution we would still have the problem of the blackness of our sin. If we balanced the world's ecosystem, we would not prevent the destruction of the world. It is inevitable. There will be a day when this world and the things of it will pass away, but for those whose names are written in the book of life, there will be a new heaven and a new earth.

And I heard a great voice out of heaven saying, Behold, the tabernacle of God is with men, and He will dwell with them, and they shall be His people, and God Himself shall be with them, and be their God. And God shall wipe away all tears from their eyes; and there shall be no more death, neither sorrow, nor crying, neither shall there be any more pain: for the former things are passed away. And He that sat upon the throne said, Behold, I make all things new. And He said unto me, Write:

147

for these words are true and faithful. And He said unto me, It is done. I am the Alpha and Omega, the beginning and the end. I will give unto him that is athirst of the fountain of the water of life freely. He that overcometh shall inherit all things; and I will be his God, and he shall be my son. But the fearful, and unbelieving, and the abominable, and murderers, and whoremongers, and sorcerers, and idolaters, and all liars, shall have their part in the lake which burneth with fire and brimstone: which is the second death. Revelations 21:3-8

What a wonderful place God will create. No more sin, no more bickering, no more people arguing over senseless arguments. No more fear of retribution. God will make all things new. Imagine a city of pure gold, garnished with all manner of precious stones where you can live in perfect peace.

And the nations of them which are saved shall walk in the light of it: and the kings of the earth do bring their glory and honour into it.And the gates of it shall not be shut at all by day: for there shall be no night there.And they shall bring the glory and honour of the nations into it.And there shall in no wise enter into it any thing that defileth, neither whatsoever worketh abomination, or maketh a lie: but they which are written in the Lamb's book of life. Revelations 21:22-27

What a marvelous place this will be to live. A perfect place.

This planet is coming to an end. We can't stop that; the course has already been set. However, we can have a part in directing the souls of mankind to the Savior. In doing so, if they receive God's gift of salvation, they too will have their names written in the Lamb's book of life and will enjoy the blessings of a new heaven and a new earth.

But the heavens and the earth, which are now, by the same word are kept in store, reserved unto fire against the day of judgment and perdition of ungodly men. But, beloved, be not ignorant of this one thing, that one day is with the Lord as a thousand years, and a thousand years as one day. The Lord is not slack concerning His promise, as some men count slackness; but is longsuffering to us-ward, not willing that any should perish, but that all should come to repentance. II Peter 3:7-9

For myself, I'm looking to that new earth and praying for those who don't have their names written in the Lamb's book of life, that they might seek God and put their trust in Jesus Christ for the forgiveness of sins and the salvation of their souls. In finding Him and trusting in Him, they will also receive the blessing of the coming new heaven and new earth.

Faith by Works or Works by Faith

"shew me thy faith without thy works, and I will shew thee my faith by my works." James 2:18

"Knowing that a man is not justified by the works of the law, but by the faith of Jesus Christ, even we have believed in Jesus Christ, that we might be justified by the faith of Christ, and not by the works of the law: for by the works of the law shall no flesh be justified." Galatians 2:16

The Puritans sought to base the laws of this country on the Bible: an admirable pursuit. In their efforts to do so, they brought upon people in the colonies a governorship that required individuals to follow their laws of worship.

The Puritans lived exemplary, godly lives. However, in their fervor to build a country on godliness; they overstepped the freedom God gave us, the ability to choose to believe. This, in my mind, raises the question of their understanding of being saved by grace.

God's Word tells us to live out our faith, but it is important that we first have faith in the Truth. Many people start attending a church and begin to play the role of a Christian, yet have they embraced faith in the death, burial and resurrection of Jesus Christ for the redemption of their sins, or do they trust in their works to save them? Some live in such a manner that they put truly born again believers to shame—but without faith it is impossible to please God.

While living a good life is important and can be fruitful for our time on earth, it can never be enough to cover the debt of our sins.

Without understanding that our sin keeps us from a right relationship with God, and without understanding that each one of us is born with a sinful nature, we, as individuals, cannot grasp the need for redemption.

The Puritans wanted to keep the colonies free from evil and corruption, yet in doing so they persecuted individuals who sought to preach the Gospel to those who needed faith. Today I see the opposite happening. I find many churches are afraid to give the Gospel straight from the Bible. Instead of seeking godliness, as the Puritans did, they seek to fit into the world. They have chosen the path of faith without works to the extent they eliminate from their message the need for repentance.

People need to live their faith, but they cannot successfully live it without first having it. As Christians, we must show our faith by our works, and take care that we also present the Gospel, the foundation of our faith. By presenting the Gospel and clearly stating that the wrong things we do keep us from a Holy God, we can help individuals see that faith in their works will get them nowhere.

It is time to move away from the fear of offense and preach sin as sinful. Yet, balance this with the behavior of one having received the grace of salvation for one's own sin. We cannot force another to have faith by making them obey laws. The Pharisees taught us this. However, we can live in such a way that we draw others to Christ, humbly recognizing that without the shedding of His blood on the cross there would be no hope for us to have a right relationship with God.

He Spared Not His Own Son

"He that spared not His own Son, but delivered Him up for us all, how shall He not with Him also freely give us all things?" Romans 8:32

Could there be any greater gift than Christ crucified for us—a perfect God, giving up the holiness and sanctity of Heaven, coming down to a corrupt world in order to save us from ultimate destruction? There cannot. Therefore, there is no reason that God could not give us all things.

God loves us. He would not withhold good from us. Sometimes what we think is good, is not, and sometimes what we think is not good is. God chastises us or allows seemingly bad things to enter our lives not because He is incapable or unloving. On the contrary, in verse 29 He clearly states He allows these things to come into our lives so that we will be conformed to the image of His Son ("For whom He did foreknow, He also did predestinate to be conformed to the image of His Son, that He might be the firstborn among many brethren.")

The Jews and Christians at the time Paul penned this did not have the easy life we have today. They experienced persecution and hate (Romans 8:17-18), but God wanted them to know that it is not because He is not capable of giving them relief and good things. Rather, He wanted them to see these things as an opportunity to grow. He wanted them, and us, to know that we are more than conquerors through Him. He wanted them to look at things from an eternal perspective and on the spiritual plane. In all their horrendous sufferings, Paul was convinced, first that he had received the ultimate gift in Christ, and second that nothing could separate him from the love of God, which is in Christ Jesus. To God be all glory, and honor, and praise.

Are You Good Enough?

"For since by man came death, by man came also the resurrection of the dead. For as in Adam all die, even so in Christ shall all be made alive." I Corinthians 15:22-23

The origin of man's sinful nature began in the Garden of Eden. It began in the heart of one person. It began when that person decided to disobey a seemingly simple command not to eat the fruit of the Tree of the Knowledge of Good and Evil.

So horrendous was that one decision in the eyes of the Holy God that He expelled Adam and Eve from His presence. No longer could they walk with Him; no longer could they partake in the bounty of God's garden; no longer could they eat of the Tree of Life (Genesis 3).

That one incident of giving into temptation led to the demise of mankind. Murder ensued, wars erupted, hatred reigned, and greed led humans down paths of great impoverishment. One little decision, as simple as deciding to steal a cookie from the cookie jar; as easy as taking pens home from the office: this one decision changed the course of mankind.

The Holiest of Beings cannot stand the sight of sin (I Samuel 2:2). In His presence not even a speck of rebellion must exist. Yet God was not finished with humanity. He knew man's fall would happen and in His great love He designed a plan. A plan that would send rippling affects through the ages; a plan that would result in a separation from the world and its course of destruction while forming an unbreakable bond with those who receive it.

Today, when a person dies, it is common to hear "he was a good person." Implicit with this saying is the understanding that such a person would surely go to Heaven. However, if Adam and Eve were expelled from God's presence for one simple act of taking what they were told not to, is there anyone (with the exception of Christ) so good as to not have committed so 'slight' a sin? The Bible tells us there is not (Romans 3:23). The measure of goodness for the entrance to Heaven is by God's standards, not ours. No one is good enough to enter through its gates.

Though Adam and Eve offered sacrifices to God, they were never again allowed into the Garden of Eden. Closed to them forever, their now sin-diseased bodies would experience death. However, God, in His infinite wisdom and love, saw fit to make a way for us to once again join in fellowship with Him.

Our sins, be they small or great, separate us from God. Death became the end result (Romans 6:23). Howbeit through the death of one perfect, sinless man, we can have our fellowship with God restored. Jesus, God the Son, died on the cross, bringing upon His perfect, sinless self all our sins (II Corinthians 5:21). He paid the price of death for us. He conquered death when, after being buried for three days and three nights, He rose from the grave, and later ascended to His Father in Heaven (I Corinthians 15:3-4).

Eternal life was lost in the Garden of Eden (Genesis 3:33): lost for each person who has ever committed even the smallest sin. Only one pathway is possible to restore that eternal life: for someone sinless to die in our place. While here on earth our flesh, our body, is dead; but for those who turn from the course of natural man and call upon Jesus, the Savior, accepting His payment, His death in place of ours, eternal life is found. Those who believe will one day again be able to eat of the Tree of Life in Heaven (Revelations 22:2) and live with God.

Spiritual Life

Everyone has a spirit—it is that part of you that needs to connect with someone beyond yourself in a very intimate fashion, and on a level beyond normal human communication.

People try to bring their spirit to life in many ways. Some seek a kinship with others. Some use material possession to extend themselves, replacing the need for a spiritual connection. Some seek it through religion. Whatever the case, everyone desires to have his or her spirit quickened (to restore to life).

Those who acknowledge that something is missing in their lives begin to seek fulfillment. They may not say that they feel spiritually dead; they may not even be aware they have a spirit. Nonetheless everyone will have a moment in his or her life where a dullness, an emptiness, a feeling of being alone, will spark realization of a need. Some may only acknowledge it for a moment. Others will spend years of their lives seeking after it. Still others will discover a quickening of their spirit that brings such great joy and peace and that changes their inner thoughts, feelings, and attitudes—they become a new creature.

Where are you? Did you know that there is a way to make your spirit alive? No, it is not through the conjuring up of spirits. It is not through religion and religious rites. It is not through a kinship with other people, nor through the gathering of wealth and possessions.

There is only one way, and that is through Jesus Christ, known also as the Word, God's Son, Creator. A simple act of disobedience killed the connection mankind had with the Holy Spirit, that is, with God. One great act, the sacrifice of Jesus Christ, made reconnection possible.

The Bible says:

But God, who is rich in mercy, for His great love wherewith He loved us, Even when we were dead in sins, hath quickened us together with Christ, (by grace ye are saved;) And hath raised us up together, and made us sit together in heavenly places in Christ Jesus: That in the ages to come He might shew the exceeding riches of His grace in His kindness toward us through Christ Jesus. (Ephesians 2:4-7)

The work has been done. The gift is offered. The price is paid. Only acknowledge your need and believe.

For whosoever shall call upon the name of the Lord shall be saved. Romans 10:13

Good News the World Needs to Hear

*Moreover, brethren, I declare unto you the **Gospel** which I preached unto you, which also ye have received, and wherein ye stand; By which also ye are **saved**, if ye keep in memory what I preached unto you, unless ye have believed in vain. For I delivered unto you first of all that which I also received, how that **Christ died for our sins** according to the scriptures; And that He was **buried**, and that **He rose again** the third day according to the scriptures:* I Corinthians 15:1-4 *(KJV)*

The world needs to hear that we are the enemies of the Creator of this world. It also needs to hear that we can have peace with Him through the death, burial and resurrection of His only begotten Son, Jesus Christ.

The wickedness of our lives has separated us from God and taken us to a place of eternal damnation.

And Who is it that can save us? No one but Jesus Christ, God's Son. Death is the end result of sin, but life is given to those who chose to believe that Jesus, God's Son, died for our sins, was buried, and conquered death when He rose again. He was the perfect sacrifice, offered for the forgiveness of our sins that we might live; not as slaves to our sins, but as freed men, living by the faith and grace of our Lord and Savior.

And what should we do to be saved?

Sirs, what must I do to be saved? And they said, Believe on the Lord Jesus Christ, and thou shalt be saved, and thy house. Acts 16:30-31

That if thou shalt confess with thy mouth the Lord Jesus, and shalt believe in thine heart that God hath raised Him from the dead, thou shalt be saved. For with the heart man believeth unto righteousness; and with the mouth confession is made unto salvation. For the Scripture saith, Whosoever believeth on Him shall not be ashamed. For there is no difference between the Jew and the Greek: for the same Lord over all is rich unto all that call upon Him. For whosoever shall call upon the name of the Lord shall be saved. Romans 10:9-13 *(KJV)*

So pray to God acknowledging that you are a sinner in need of His salvation; ask for forgiveness; confess your faith in His Son, Jesus Christ and that you believe He died, was buried and rose again; and receive His free gift of salvation.

- Now tell someone about it—you can email me at lynnsquire@gmail.com
- Now study the Bible so that you may know Who has saved you and learn all about God, Who has given such a great sacrifice that He might have a relationship with you.
- Now attend a Bible-believing, Gospel-preaching Church.
- Now pray every day.

Study to shew thyself approved unto God, a workman that needeth not to be ashamed, rightly dividing the word of truth. II Timothy 2:15

The Four Spiritual Laws

1. You are a sinner (Romans 3:23)
2. You must pay a price for your sin (Romans 6:23)
3. Salvation comes by accepting and believing the fact that Jesus paid the price for your sins when He died, was buried, and rose from the grave, and that He is the only way of salvation (Romans 5:8 and John 3:16)
4. You must call upon Jesus to save you. (Romans 10:13)

My Thoughts on Life

There is nothing quite like knowing where you are going. As a believer that Jesus Christ is the Son of God, and that He died, was buried, and rose again in order to save me from my sins, I know where I will be the moment my life here on earth is ended. As a wife, I know what is expected of me from God, and occasionally from my husband (whom I love and cherish very much). As a mother, I know that my life and the lives of my children are in the hands of an all-powerful, all-knowing, ever-present, eternal, holy, just, and loving Creator. As an author, I am compelled to see the world, not through man's eyes, not even through my eyes, but through the eyes of an all-seeing God, as He exposes it and His plans for it in His Holy Word.

My life becomes defined, not by what I believe about myself (because I know that my heart, despite my efforts, is deceitful), but by the Creator's hand as He works within me to mold me into a new creation. So, though I have the freedom to make my own decisions (and therefore my own mistakes), I know that ultimately I am held in the hands of Someone more wise than myself, more knowledgeable, more righteous, and more powerful than myself. This security propels me into a life guided by God's holy, perfect, and eternal Word, and the adventures, trials, blessings, and riches such a life presents.

Like many women my age I wear a number of different hats, and so when someone asks me to describe who I am, I wonder which hat that person is seeing me wear. The first and foremost hat that I wear is one as a child of God, saved by grace; my second hat is as a wife, then a mother, an author, a business person, a church member, a daughter, a sister, and a friend. But while all those hats are different, they are still on my head, and the makeup of my personality, history, culture, and experiences are what make me uniquely me no matter what I wear. So here is a bit of history, culture, and a few traits that make up my character description.

I grew up on a farm in that wonderful and somewhat undiscovered part of the world of Arrowwood, Alberta, Canada. While most kids in those days may have travelled to their friend's place on foot or on a bike, I made my wanderings on horseback. I have phenomenal memories of grand adventures experienced from the back of my valiant steeds.

So much of who I am comes from this experience and from the love I have for the history of Alberta and for the history of my family. Much of my culture is passed down to me from an ancestry filled with pioneers and pilgrims of noble character, great fortitude, and a love for God. They braved persecution and hardship with a hope for the future of a better land. I enjoy the freedoms and luxuries of life because of these extraordinary, hardworking people.

However, even more of my personal make-up comes from a realization as a child that I was a sinner in need of a Savior. In the back room of our small country church, under the guidance of a faithful young woman desiring to serve the Lord herself, I laid my life down at the cross, and accepted the forgiveness of sins and the life Jesus Christ offered to me. This was a day of transformation. Though I am a work in progress, my life from that day forward had a purpose, changing the course of my future. I accepted this testimony from my Lord and Savior, Jesus Christ, and now I rejoice in the knowledge of His abundant grace in my life.

Because of my love for Christ I found myself drawn into His ministry, and for a great number of years that ministry was in camping. At children's camps throughout Western Canada I savored the unique position of leading many children through the same decision I made as a child.

Before I turned thirty the Lord decided to bless me with a wonderful man for a husband. God then drew us away from Canada and into California, where we now reside with our three children. His ever guiding hand brought us to a wonderful God-fearing, Bible-believing church in which we have been blessed to have many opportunities to use our God-given gifts.

Cherubim and the Cross

In Exodus God gave Moses instructions on how to build the Tabernacle. These included making golden cherubim in the two ends of the mercy seat, and cherubim on the veil.

The cherubim would be a symbol to the Israelites—a reminder that when they entered the tabernacle, they were entering into the presence of God.

What reminds us we are entering into the presence of God? The Cross, of course! We cannot come before God without first coming to the cross.

Not until we have laid our sins at the cross, that is, on Jesus who bore our sins on the cross, burying our old selves with Him in the grave, can we rise up with Christ into the presence of God.

We who have done so have received the Holy Spirit and are continually in the presence of God—our bodies become that tabernacle (I Corithians 3:16). What a truly awesome fact.

Pray without Ceasing

"And He spake a parable unto them to this end, that men ought always to pray, and not to faint;" Luke 18:1

Jesus' crucifixion drew near, and the disciples had much to learn. They needed to persist in prayer with faith. They needed to learn to never give up on God. God would hear, and He would respond.

Jesus mentioned persistence which indicates that God appears silent at times, and our prayers seem unheard. Often an eternity seems to pass before an answer is given, but for God it is shorter than a blink of an eye.

Our finite minds cannot fathom the workings of our God—a God who created us and all things. God times His answer to the rhythm of His great masterpiece. Our request may be only one staccato note in the entire cantata and His answer must come only in its perfect timing. Enjoy His performance; pray, listen, and wait.

For further study: Luke 18:1-8; Psalm 88, 89; Ecclesiastes 11:1-6

Thought for the Day: Only God sends the wind to blow the sails of your ship.

Meditation verse: Romans 8:26 "Likewise the Spirit also helpeth our infirmities: for we know not what we should pray for as we ought: but the Spirit itself maketh intercession for us with groanings which cannot be uttered."

The Prayer Closet

Jesus taught us how to pray in Matthew 6:5-13. Find a quiet place, a prayer closet (Matthew 6:6), and prepare your heart to become intimate with God. You are coming before the throne of grace (Hebrews 4:16).

The following is a guide based on Matthew 6 that you can use to strengthen your prayer life:

- Acknowledge who He is.
- Acknowledge your relationship with Him. He is your Savior; you are His redeemed. He is your Father; you are His child.
- Adore Him. Praise Him for His attributes; His love, His grace, His mercy, His holiness, His righteousness, His awesome power, etc.
- Acknowledge His sovereignty. He is sovereign over all creation, both physical and spiritual.
- Acknowledge His will. Do you desire to do it?
- Now make your requests and petitions known to Him. Pray for your family, your church, missionaries, those who are not saved, and for those you will be in touch with throughout the day. Then pray for your personal needs.
- Evaluate your relationships with others. Is there someone you have offended? Have you wronged someone? Are you fighting with someone? Confess these before God and determine to make right these relationships according to God's guidance.

- Ask for forgiveness for any sins the Lord has made known to you and determine to repent, turning away from them.
- Ask for His guidance, perhaps on how to overcome problems, or on where He wants you to go.
- Acknowledge your weaknesses. What do you struggle with? What are you afraid of?
- Ask for victory over those weaknesses and leave them with Him.
- Praise Him, thank Him, and commit yourself to Him, resting in the knowledge of who He is.

Return to Me and I Will Return to You

"Then they that feared the Lord spake often one to another: and the Lord hearkened, and heard it, and a book of remembrance was written before Him for them that feared the Lord, and that thought upon His name." Malachi 3:16

While sharing good byes with my mentoring group at the Mount Hermon Writers' Conference, the instructor said, "They will know you are a Christian by how you live."

I never had a chance to get clarification. I wasn't even sure if it was a general statement or pointed specifically at me. In context, it seemed a statement that applied to the general populous. However, it nagged me. I couldn't help but think it was for me, and the question that kept coming up was: Could people tell I am a Christian by how I live?

I don't consider myself a bad person. My days consist of many good acts. No time is spent doing drugs, alcohol, or going to bars. Yet, I found myself needled by the comment.

Upon returning home, life stepped into a normal high pace of activity. Yet that one statement nagged me at every turn and in every moment with God.

Weary from the endless number of duties to fulfill, I found my heart grew numb. Instead of listening to the speakers through the missions' conference at our church, I found myself captured by a verse in each session and compelled to study it out. A change was needed, but I didn't know where to begin.

Then I read Malachi 3. God revealed the coming of Christ. He said the Christ would be a refiner and purifier. He told of the judgments to come, and called for the Israelites to return to Him.

In verses 13 to 15, the people give "stout" words against God. They revealed their hard hearts: the bitterness that comes when hardships assail even when a consequence of their sin.

God's response to their words was a description of those He calls His own. These are people that fear Him. These people meet together with others that fear Him, and they pray. They think on His name.

What caught my attention was that by observing the lives of those that fear Him, the Israelites would return to Him. Not only would they return to Him, but they would "discern between the righteous and the wicked, between him that serveth God and him that serveth Him not." (verse 18).

This hit home. How can people know I am a Christian? I fear God; I fellowship with others that fear God; I pray with those that fear God; and I think upon His name. That is my light, my beacon on a hill. May those around me see and be drawn to Jesus Christ, our Lord and Savior.

A Guide to Studying the Bible

If you want to know someone you need to spend time with him, listening to what he has to say. The same is true with God. If you want to know God, you need to study the Bible, His Holy Word.

Here is a list of things you can do that will help you dig a little deeper into His Word:

- Pray for God's guidance and help in understanding.
- Chose a book to study (for example Philemon).
- Read the book through in one sitting.
- Note the time period it was written, who wrote it (e.g. Paul wrote Philemon), the setting (where), and to whom the book was written.
- Make notes on any specific geographic and cultural aspects that affect the "characters".
- Determine the book's theme or purpose.
- Discover the key verse—the verse that explains why the book was written or holds the main point of the book.
- Divide the book into sections according to the main themes discussed.
- Divide the sections into scenes and/or paragraphs.
- For each section ask who, what, where, why, when and how.
- Mark any key words—words that are used repeatedly or hold special significance to the theme of the book.
- Note any lists—these will hold significance in the overall topic discussed in the section or entire book.

- Breakdown the structure of key sentences or complex sentences. Note what the subject, verbs, and objects are. Note what adverbs are applied to what verbs and what adjectives describe what nouns (subject or object).
- Determine what actions the characters were to take in their lives based on the instructions in the passage.
- Determine how the passage applies to you.
- Pray God will help you apply the precepts and principles you have learned from this book.

Although you can study the Bible on your own, here is a list of some useful study helps:

- Dictionary
- Concordance
- Book on Biblical history and culture
- Bible Atlas

Keep a notebook with your Bible so you can jot down what you learned and refer to it throughout your study.

A Brief Look at the Virtuous Woman

The world today drives women to be like men, giving little room for men to have anything left of their manhood and women to be true women. Women's rights are touted by some with the fervor of evangelists. With little deference to their unique creation and a continual advocation for irresponsible freedom, these "evangelists" lose the grace, beauty, and selflessness of a true woman.

Yet God's description of a true woman silences those evangelists. He gives us His example of real womanhood in Proverbs 31:10-31. This is the example every Christian woman should strive to follow. A brief look at the virtuous woman, the one God has told us to strive to be, follows.

"Who can find a virtuous woman? For her price is far above rubies. The heart of her husband doth safely trust in her, so that he shall have no need of spoil. She will do him good and not evil all the days of her life." Proverbs 31:10-12

From a business perspective, this woman is the perfect employee—good business sense, reliable, and trustworthy. She has a good relationship with those beneath her and with those she serves. A hard worker, she is diligent and goes beyond the call of duty.

This woman is not reliant on her husband to meet her needs ("he shall have no need of spoil"). This woman, as we shall see in later verses, is capable of providing for the needs of her family. A pillar of strength and wisdom, she is careful with her husband's money and inheritance such that he does not need to go out and obtain more than what he currently has.

"She seeketh wool, and flax, and worketh willingly with her hands. She is like the merchants ships; she bringeth her food from afar." Proverbs 31:13-14

This woman is a "power shopper". She knows precisely what she needs to care for her household, and she settles for nothing less than a good deal. Like a merchant ship in search of good product at a bargain, she will go the extra mile to get the best at a good price. She knows what materials she needs for her products (which she sells in verse 24) and seeks it out, working willingly to create the best.

"She riseth also while it is yet night, and giveth meat to her household, and a portion to her maidens." Proverbs 31:15

This woman cares for her household, including her servants. Who are the servants of today? Dishwashers, stoves, microwaves, kitchen appliances replace the kitchen help of ancient times. Washing machines, dryers, vacuum cleaners, and other cleaning machines replace the housekeepers of the past. If this woman lived today, she would take care in her use of these modern conveniences and ensure they receive the proper maintenance and repairs they need.

"She considereth a field, and buyeth it: with the fruit of her hands she planteth a vineyard." Proverbs 31:16

Agriculture was the major industry of that day and this woman excelled at it. In those days property was inherited by the son (although a woman could inherit if there was no son). Fields were rarely sold and to have the ability to buy a field indicated wealth. This woman was prosperous, and by all indication she prospered by the work of her own hand.

"She girdeth her loins with strength, and strengtheneth her arms." Proverbs 31:17

This woman did not live on the verge of exhaustion. Her family and her servants probably never heard her say "I'm so tired today." She took care of her health and likely did not complain about little aches or pains or illnesses.

"She perceiveth that her merchandise is good: her candle goeth not out by night." Proverbs 31:18

This woman was a top notch business woman. She knew that what she did made good profit, both financially and in the care of her household. The product of her work was pleasant and agreeable. She was prepared to work 24/7 for her household. There was no 'me' time when the 'shop' was closed. She was prepared to work any time of the day or night, and she was available for her family any time of the day or night.

"She layeth her hands to the spindle, and her hands hold the distaff." Proverbs 31:19

As noted before, this woman was a hard worker. She met her family's needs. There is a sense that she was tireless in her diligence; so great was her love for her family that she persisted in her work. Selflessly giving, she likely found her pleasure in seeing her family's needs met and exceeded.

"She stretcheth out her hand to the poor; yea, she reacheth forth her hands to the needy." Proverbs 31:20

Although focused on the care of her family, this woman had compassion on others. She did not keep to herself, staying away from the needs of her community. This woman was generous, kind, perhaps merciful, and certainly gracious. These simple acts speak volumes. This woman, though very busy and a hard worker, took the time, energy, and resources to be good to others. Her husband saw it; her children saw it. I am sure these same traits were directed to her family.

"She is not afraid of the snow for her household: for all her household are clothed with scarlet." Proverbs 31:21

When hardships came, this woman's household did not suffer as others. She prepared for those times. Scarlet was a symbol of wealth. So well did she provide, that her household experienced wealth in times of hardship.

"She maketh herself coverings of tapestry; her clothing is silk and purple." Proverbs 31:22

Tapestries were used on walls as a form of insulation. When worn, they would be moved to beds for coverings, and eventually to floors to provide insulation there. Tapestries were also a form of decorating. Again, we see this woman ensuring the needs of her household were well met. Not only this, but she cared for the appearance of her home, decorating it and making it warm and inviting.

In her clothing, this woman demonstrated wealth and position. She cared about her appearance as much as she cared about the appearance of her home.

"Her husband is known in the gates, when he sitteth among the elders of the land." Proverbs 31:23

So competent was this woman that her husband was able to excel. To sit at the gates as one of the elders was a position of rank. He was among the judges and the officers. He had no need to worry about his personal finances and the well being of his home because his wife successfully took care of them.

"She maketh fine linen, and selleth it; and delivereth girdles unto the merchant." Proverbs 31:24

Certainly her husband need not worry about his family finances; his wife was a business woman. What she made at home, she took to the merchant who would sell it for her.

"Strength and honour are her clothing; and she shall rejoice in time to come." Proverbs 31:25

Her perseverance in life, her personal fortitude, these distinguished her from the rest. She was a force worthy of praise. She was bold, mighty, and powerful. This woman wore a beautiful inner character, a character most excellent. She did not fear the future because her past and present life would bring her glory and would provide for her needs in her old age.

"She openeth her mouth with wisdom; and in her tongue is the law of kindness. She looketh well to the ways of her household, and eateth not the bread of idleness. Her children arise up, and call her blessed; her husband also, and he praiseth her." Proverbs 31:26-28

This woman was people oriented. She cared for others, and she knew that wisdom and kindness were partners in this care. Her family loved her and thought very highly of her. She was a blessing to those for whom she loved and cared.

"Many daughters have done virtuously, but thou excellest them all." Proverbs 31:29

This woman demonstrated the ability to be a one person army. She showed great strength and discipline in her labors, and was a storehouse of godly character. Her interactions with people proved her valor. She was resourceful, strong, powerful, and efficient.

"Favour is deceitful, and beauty is vain: but a woman that feareth the Lord, she shall be praised." Proverbs 31:30

Her success came from the simple fact of her fear of the Lord. In awe of the Almighty, and in knowledge of His righteous judgment, this woman's life demonstrated her faith.

"Give her of the fruit of her hands; and let her own works praise her in the gates." Proverbs 31:31

She had no need to boast of her abilities and accomplishments. They spoke for her. The men in town who sat at the gates knew she excelled—her husband helped, I'm sure, in his praise of her.

To embrace God's description of a true woman is to seek to excel in godly living. A woman who lives as this virtuous woman did will experience success, not as the world views success, but as God does—such a woman will be able to "rejoice in time to come."

Women of Noble Character

Who can find a virtuous woman? For her price is far above rubies.
Proverbs 31:10

A woman with a noble character will always put her family before her career and before herself. Her self-image comes not from her career, nor from the outward success of her family. She proves herself in her service to those she loves. Strangers recognize her virtue because of how she conducts herself in business and because of her generosity. She is noted for her willingness to help others. Provision for her family is her highest priority. Her family is well cared for, and it shows. The key behind her success as a wife and mother is her fear of God.

Further Study: Proverbs 31:10-31; I Timothy 2:9-15; 3:11; 5:16; Titus 2:1-5; I Peter 3:1-6

Food for Thought: Live in such a way that the world cannot speak evil of the Word of God.

Bodily Exercise versus Godliness

For bodily exercise profiteth little: but godliness is profitable unto all things, having promise of the life that now is, and of that which is to come. I Timothy 4:8

With the extensive food allergies and other health problems that I have I must be extremely disciplined in order to maintain a certain quality of life. A mere slip of self-control can send me into a downward spiral that ends with me either gasping for breath or curled up on my bed, wreathing in pain and begging for mercy. Abstinence from certain foods and activities is a way of survival.

In Ephesus, during Paul's day, many people sought to attain a higher spiritual plane through asceticism, or bodily exercise. Paul warned Timothy that in latter days people would abstain from certain foods or marriage, etc. as a part of their spiritual walk. He said such teachings came from seducing spirits and doctrines of devils.

Today I see people going on diets to attain bodily perfection or in search of a better quality of life. Sometimes their lives depend on it, but often it is out of a desire to meet society's expectation of looks and health. The Bible, however, teaches that such disciplines profit little.

Bodily exercise, or asceticism, is mankind struggling to attain a level of life (spiritual or physical) that is not possible to achieve. It is an attempt to meet a need they alone cannot satisfy. However, the Bible says that "godliness is profitable unto all things."

Godliness is holiness. It is a reverence and respect toward God. The mystery of godliness is defined in I Timothy 3:16 "God was manifested in the flesh, justified in the Spirit, seen of angels, preached unto the Gentiles, believed on in the world, received up into glory." Faith in this mystery is what brings about godliness. A sincere and deep reverence for God leads a person into living a life that pleases Him. Thus godliness has "the promise of the life that now is, and of that which is to come."

Merely going through the motions of living "rightly" is not sufficient. Godliness is; and godliness is attained through faith (Titus 3:5; Ephesians 2:8-9).

There is nothing wrong with dieting and exercise. There is nothing wrong with abstaining from certain activities and foods. However, relying on these disciplines to bring you a quality of life that only faith in the Lord Jesus Christ can give you is to believe a lie.

Let's take this a step further. Our perception of quality of life is wrong. We think that if we have all our wants met—if we are thin enough, beautiful enough, fit enough, healthy enough, etc.—that we will receive a sense of well-being, peace, and joy. But these temporal things only produce the illusion of such qualities. True peace and joy, true quality of life comes from trusting God.

If we pursue fitness, wealth, beauty, and even attain it, does it last when funds start coming? Does it last when cruel words hurt us, or sudden illness overtakes us? No, the sense of well-being, the peace, and the joy brought about by meeting the desires of our bodies and imaginations does not last through trials. What does last is God's peace and joy.

The attainment of true peace and true joy *may* actually involve suffering reproach, loss of life, and poverty, because in these things we can see God at work; He shows us that He is Lord. Relying on Him to sustain us, we can reach the spiritual plane where peace rests not on what we do, or what we can obtain (which will fall away), but on an Eternal, All-Powerful, All-Knowing God. Here we find true joy: a joy founded not on possessions or looks, but on a right relationship with our Creator. To God be all glory, honor, and praise.

A Forgiving and Generous Nature

I believe God often uses nature and animals to teach us something (Job 12:7 *But ask now the beasts, and they shall teach thee; and the fowls of the air, and they shall tell thee:*). Horses are no exception.

Over the years I've watched trail horses plod along underneath the unsympathetic weight of a novice or first time rider. Such a rider may be stiff, jarring his seat against the poor horse's back. Yet the faithful animal jogs along, paying no heed to the pain that may be growing along its spine.

I have seen horses nuzzle a rider after a long, grueling day's ride, acting as though the person had been feeding it sugar cubes all day. Forgiving the rider for mistakes he made like jarring the horse's mouth or kicking its sides, it relishes in the relief brought by a grooming without rehashing past tortures.

I wonder sometimes how willing I would be to put up with the abuse a faithful, old trail horse does. When I am faced with requests that seem pointless and meaningless, do I faithfully obey? If I was told to do one thing, but punished for not doing what the rider thought he told me to do, would I allow that person to remain on my back? Have I ever allowed a thoughtless person to continue to hurt me without complaint?

Yes, I think there is much I could learn about the forgiving and generous nature of a horse.

Miraculous Aliens

Take heed to yourselves, that your heart be not deceived, and ye turn aside, and serve other gods, and worship them; Deuteronomy 11:16 (KJV)

In previous centuries and other cultures, stories told gave listeners insight into the beliefs and traditions of their society. A few years ago, after the release of a new science fiction movie, I sat in a public area and overheard a conversation that caught my interest and made me ponder the above statement in relation to our own society.

Two women discussed archaeological findings in the Middle East that suggested Moses' encounters with God were really encounters with aliens. One woman quoted from a book she read regarding such encounters and the other could offer no other explanation—perhaps Jesus was an alien after all?

I huffed at the discussion. I never considered such Biblical accounts like "Moses and the Burning Bush" an encounter with an alien. From my perspective the conversation spoke of heresy, and a lie contrived by Satan himself. Then it occurred to me that the premise of most science fiction movies was the existence of life in other galaxies and on other planets. If you took God out of the equation how else could you explain the miraculous phenomena of the Bible?

Two hundred years ago the vast majority of people in the Western World did not believe in encounters with aliens from a different planet. Today the possibility of such an encounter is an expectation. If

"Hollywood" has become our society's storyteller, does it not make sense that today people would believe such things?

Perhaps then, we have a responsibility to change. We could change the storyteller we listen to, or we could attempt to change the storyteller. I believe there is a little of both going on today but whatever we do, we must be certain to do it not under the guidance of an alien, but of the Holy Spirit. Change will not be effective unless the change is God-driven and God-endorsed.

Testimony

Every person who is saved can tell of a time in their life when he realized he is a horrible person and needed rescuing. This realization, if met with the Gospel, may have led that person to bow down before the Lord Jesus Christ believing that God made Jesus the perfect sacrifice, the payment for all the evil deeds he has ever done and will ever do. At the moment of this belief a person can have the assurance that when he dies he will be with the Lord Jesus in Heaven (what a glorious day that will be). Each person who is saved will recall this day (though he may not remember the time or date) and can rejoice.

I have had such a time in my life. When I was five years old I came home from Sunday School and sat on my bed. I prayed at that time that I would one day be with Jesus. I did not understand all that was involved, but I knew that was what I wanted.

About two years later, I was answering questions in a Mailbox Club handout from Vacation Bible School. A question caused me great concern; when were you saved? I thought I was saved, but I couldn't be sure and I knew I needed to get this point settled. I could not wait until I could ask my teacher how I could be sure I was saved.

The next day I stayed after VBS, and the teacher took me through the Wordless Book, a book that illustrates by use of colors how a person can be saved. She showed me the black page and said how this represented my sin, all those bad things I had done. She quoted Romans 3:23 "For all have sinned and come short of the glory of God."

She then showed me a red page. She quoted Romans 6:23 "For the wages of sin is death, but the gift of God is eternal life through

Jesus Christ our Lord." She told me that the debt of my sin needed to be paid for, so Jesus shed His blood by dying on the cross for my sin. He died, was buried, and rose again.

The white page, I was told, represented my heart if I asked Jesus to forgive me of my sins and come into my heart. The black page showed the condition of my heart, but should I be saved, Jesus would wash me clean. Psalm 51:7 says "...Wash me, and I shall be whiter than snow."

She then turned to a gold page and said that this page represented the streets of gold found in Heaven. She told me that there was only one way to get to Heaven, and that was through faith in Jesus Christ. John 14:6 "Jesus saith unto him, I am the way, the truth, and the life, no man cometh unto the Father but by me."

I then prayed with her and accepted Jesus Christ as my personal savior.

Afterward the teacher showed me the green page and said this represented the growth a Christian should have. I took all of this to heart and I know that my life changed from that moment on.

I have eternal security; I know for certain that when I die I will go to Heaven, because of what the Bible says:

That if thou shalt confess with thy mouth the Lord Jesus, and shalt believe in thine heart that God hath raised Him from the dead, thou shalt be saved.
For with the heart man believeth unto righteousness; and with the mouth confession is made unto salvation.
For the scripture saith, Whosoever believeth on Him shall not be ashamed.
For there is no difference between the Jew and the Greek: for the same Lord over all is rich unto all that call upon Him.
For whosoever shall call upon the name of the Lord shall be saved.
Romans 10:9-13

And this is the record, that God hath given to us eternal life, and this life is in His Son.
He that hath the Son hath life; and he that hath not the Son of God hath not life.
These things have I written unto you that believe on the name of the Son of God; that ye may know that ye have eternal life, and that ye may believe on the name of the Son of God. I John 5:11-13

I know that I am a miserable sinner saved by grace, but I rejoice greatly in a loving, holy heavenly Father who saw fit to give the greatest gift ever that I might be reconciled unto Him.

Perhaps you, like me have come to realize you have done bad things in your life and that you need someone to forgive you of these bad things. Perhaps you recognize that you need someone to cleanse you from your sins. Perhaps you long to know God. You too can pray and ask for His forgiveness, humbly accepting that Jesus died for your sins, was buried, and rose again conquering death. He gave His life for you, that you might have fellowship with Him. Are you willing to give your life over to Him?

If you need someone to pray with you, email me at lynnsquire@gmail.com.

1876466